USA TODAY bestselling author **Heidi Rice** lives in London, England. She is married with two teenage sons—which gives her rather too much of an insight into the male psyche—and also works as a film journalist. She adores her job, which involves getting swept up in a world of high emotion, sensual excitement, funny and feisty women, sexy and tortured men and glamorous locations where laundry doesn't exist. Once she turns off her computer she often does chores—usually involving laundry!

Growing up near the beach, **Annie West** spent lots of time observing tall, burnished lifeguards—early research! Now she spends her days fantasising about gorgeous men and their love-lives. Annie has been a reader all her life. She also loves travel, long walks, good company and great food. You can contact her at annie@annie-west.com or via PO Box 1041, Warners Bay, NSW 2282, Australia.

Discover more at millsandboon.co.uk.

REDEEMED BY MY FORBIDDEN HOUSEKEEPER

HEIDI RICE

NINE MONTHS TO SAVE THEIR MARRIAGE

ANNIE WEST

MILLS & BOON

First published in Great Britain 2023
by Mills & Boon, an imprint of HarperCollins*Publishers* Ltd,
1 London Bridge Street, London, SE1 9GF

www.harpercollins.co.uk

HarperCollins*Publishers*, Macken House, 39/40 Mayor Street Upper, Dublin 1, D01 C9W8, Ireland

Redeemed by My Forbidden Housekeeper © 2023 Heidi Rice

Nine Months to Save Their Marriage © 2023 Annie West

ISBN: 978-0-263-30692-7

09/23

This bo
For n
Printed

REDEEMED BY MY FORBIDDEN HOUSEKEEPER

HEIDI RICE

MILLS & BOON

To the babies my mum lost to miscarriage.

I still wonder who you might have been.

H x

CHAPTER ONE

Then...

Jessie

AS MY NEW heels sank into the red carpet draped over the marble steps of the eighteenth-century Palais Theatre on that late-summer evening in Paris, I felt like a princess for the first time in my life.

Cinderella, eat your heart out!

I reached into my clutch purse to retrieve the invitation which I'd 'liberated' from my cousin Belle and showed it to the doorman. My heart bounced into my throat, but the beefy guy simply smiled, and handed back the gold-embossed card—instead of declaring me an imposter and kicking me back down the marble staircase.

So far. So fabulous. Now breathe.

I sucked in an unsteady breath as I headed through the entrance hall with the rest of the glittering in-crowd and into an enormous ballroom showered with light from crystal chandeliers suspended from a painted ceiling four stories above my head.

My gaze roamed over the splendour surrounding me. Marble columns and golden statues flanked the room, while a fleet of waitstaff dressed in elegant black uniforms descended from huge twin rococo staircases, holding trays of champagne flutes and cordon bleu canapés.

Wow.

I'd left Belle and her son Cai in Nice to travel to Paris two weeks ago on the spur of the moment—I knew she needed some alone time to deal with Cai's father, Alexi Galanti—but in the past two weeks, I had also realised, now the racing team owner was back in her life, I needed to start figuring out my own future.

Belle and I had been a unit for the past four years, ever since she had turned up on my doorstep in London alone and pregnant. When her son Cai was born, we'd become a family. The first proper family I'd ever had since my mother had disappeared from my life when I was still a teenager.

But I was twenty years old now. And while I loved my job as a chef—which was something I'd trained hard at ever since I was sixteen—the long hours and complete lack of a social life had become more and more isolated. And now Belle and Cai had moved from London to Nice permanently, I knew I could no longer rely on them for company.

We would always be family. But I couldn't live vicariously through them forever.

When I had spotted the invitation to the famous masquerade ball Belle's former boss Renzo Camaro held in Paris every year, sitting discarded on her dressing table, I had popped it into my backpack on a whim—with some vague idea of using it to jump-start that process.

Belle wouldn't miss it. She'd already told me she didn't have the time, or the inclination to attend Camaro's lavish event to celebrate the start of motor racing's Super League season. And I had had some vague notion of pushing myself out of my comfort zone at last, and doing some networking, with the elite crowd Belle was a part of, because of her job as a research and development expert in the Super League. We'd talked often about me starting my own catering business, being my own boss, but I'd never had the guts to consider touting for business until now.

But as I stood under the shimmer of glittering lights, and listened to the hum of conversation as the crowd of people posed and preened in their masked finery—the vintage red satin dress I had found that afternoon after scouring every second-hand shop in the Marais cinching around my breasts and the new business cards I'd had printed burning a hole in my clutch purse—I wondered what on earth I thought I was doing here?

I was a chef. And while I might want to make a career out of cooking for people like this—one day—I'd always been on the periphery of Belle's glamorous career for a reason. Because I was the mousy cousin, who had always been happy to stay home and babysit Cai whenever Belle attended events like this one.

You're not a princess, you idiot. Or even a businesswoman. Yet. You're a fraud.

The strains of an orchestra played a Mozart serenade to welcome the guests, while the clink of champagne flutes and fine china covered the rising buzz of small talk. But the noise did nothing to drown out my thundering heartbeat. I searched the crowd— my gaze partially obscured by the gossamer mask made from scraps of antique lace—for someone I might actually know, to ease the feeling of inadequacy suddenly making my chest feel tight.

But as I looked around, even I could tell I had miscalculated. Badly. This was not the sort of place where people made business connections, or talked about them. The party vibe was far too louche and loud and—exhilarating.

Then my gaze found Renzo Camaro—our host—and

Belle's former boss, the guy who had never noticed me the few times he'd met me with my beautiful cousin. And the feeling of inadequacy threatened to crush my ribs.

He stood on the balcony above, looking like a king in his expertly tailored tuxedo. His dark hair gleamed in the sparkle of light. Lorenzo Camaro, the 'gutter rat made good' as the racing press had insisted on dubbing him ten years ago, when his Destiny Team had appeared from nowhere and taken their first Super League title.

He was still only thirty years old, even though Destiny have been at the top of the sport—vying with Alexi's Galanti team for the championship title—for over a decade. As he watched the crowd, he seemed detached and jaded, even though the stunning women on either side of him—one a supermodel, another a Hollywood starlet, both of whom I recognised—were busy flirting with him as if their lives depended on it...

Camaro was the only person not wearing a mask, making no attempt to hide the mysterious scar on his left cheek— probably because it was all part of the myth he had constructed for himself as the charming and dangerous bad boy of racing, whose notorious but vague origins in an unknown Italian slum had been whispered about for years.

The black tuxedo accentuated his height and the hard, graceful line of his muscular physique to perfection. But it was the stunning masculine beauty of his face—only made more dangerous and exciting by the scar—which captured all my attention.

A strange yearning swept through me—and the crushing weight of inadequacy dropped into my abdomen like a stone.

A hot, glowing, insistent stone.

Where the hell was that even coming from?

Camaro was so far out of my league he was practically

on Mars. Forget Mars, make that Saturn, the farthest planet from planet Jessie. And he'd never had an effect like that on me before. Probably because I had been busy fading into the furniture whenever we'd met.

And anyway, I wasn't here looking for romance. Precisely. I was here to try and kick-start a business I'd always dreamed about, but never had the guts to act on, until now.

But somehow the hot stone refused to stop glowing, and throbbing.

And a little voice in my brain began to whisper in my ear—questioning all my motivations for being here. And making the feeling of being a total imposter increase tenfold.

Had I really gone to all this trouble for professional reasons, or had it all been a naive excuse to play dress-up… And have Renzo Camaro notice me at last?

The thought was mortifying. And yet I couldn't quite dismiss it. Which only made it more mortifying, frankly.

Perhaps I should head back to the quaint bed and breakfast I'd splurged on in Montmartre? But then his hooded gaze caught mine… And stopped roaming.

My heartbeat hammered my throat and pumped wildfire deep into my abdomen, turning the damn stone into a rock of burning lava.

Oh, for pity's sake.

But even as I squirmed, far too aware of the cold satin rubbing against my oversensitized skin like sandpaper, I couldn't seem to detach my gaze from his. His eyes narrowed, and for one horrifying and unbearably exhilarating moment, as the adrenaline continued to power through my system, I thought he had actually seen me at last. And it meant something. Although I hated to think exactly what that was.

Maybe that Jessie Burton was as needy and pathetic as her mother, after all.

But before I could freak out completely, the supermodel beside Camaro broke the strange spell he seemed to have over my body by clasping his cheek and turning his face towards her. He grinned at something she said. Then tipped her chin up and placed his mouth over hers. His lips plundered, roaming over hers with an arrogant entitlement which had the breath I'd been holding releasing in a rush.

Apparently, I had been forgotten. So much for our moment of connection. It had all been in my head.

I tore my gaze away at last, feeling like the worse kind of voyeur, as he continued to devour the supermodel while enjoying the attention of the throng—who were cheering and clapping around me, having noticed the pornographic display on the balcony.

Embarrassment scoured my throat as unwanted heat made my nipples tighten painfully and my face feel as if it had been set alight.

What was that even about?

Renzo Camaro might be the hottest guy this side of Saturn, but he was also a playboy and an absolute jerk—who was well known for seducing every beautiful woman within a five-hundred-mile radius of his collossal ego.

You are not your mum. So why on earth would you want to be noticed by someone like him?

A waiter travelled through the whooping crowd carrying a tray of champagne glasses. Whipping a full glass off the tray, I took a fortifying gulp. The bubbles burst on my tongue as I ignored the cacophony around me and refused to watch Camaro and his latest conquest. From the raucous way the crowd was cheering they were obviously putting on quite a show.

Weirdly, the last thing my mother had ever said to me—before she disappeared from my life when I was fifteen—chose that precise moment to flit through my consciousness: *Never trust a good-looking man, especially one with money, baby, because you'll never be able to hold their interest for long.*

I'd always dismissed that caustic comment, because I knew she had been referring to my 'deadbeat dad'—a man she'd told me I was better off not knowing, but whom I had still always yearned to meet. But as I swallowed down the champagne, I began to wonder, perhaps that was the only honest thing she had ever told me.

Not that I wanted to attract a playboy like Camaro. Not at all. But maybe it was good to know my mum and I could agree on that much at least.

The lights dimmed and the chamber music faded, to be replaced by the bass beat of a famous rap band beginning their set in the adjoining ballroom. As people headed towards the sound, I couldn't seem to stop myself glancing back up at the balcony, but Camaro and the supermodel had disappeared.

No doubt they'd gone off to finish what they had started in the private suite he owned on the top three floors of the historic building, I decided resentfully.

Well, good riddance.

The champagne I'd drunk too fast fizzed through my bloodstream and my disappointment in Renzo and my dad, and every other guy who had failed to notice me, morphed into disgust—with myself, as much as any of them.

I placed the half-empty glass on a passing tray with trembling fingers.

You're not here to attract a guy. You're here to kick-start your catering business. And while handing out my new cards might not be the done thing, I could still at least get a close-up look at what an event like this really entailed.

I was here to do important research—and possibly some networking if the opportunity arose—for Jessie Burton Catering. But as the pounding of the bass beat began to throb in my veins and I tasted one of the canapés—a delicious roulade of spinach and smoked trout that melted on my tongue—a daring, and surprisingly exhilarating, thought bloomed inside me.

Why not enjoy myself tonight? And live the high life for a change? After all, when would I ever get the chance to attend an event like this again, with free-flowing vintage booze, an exclusive set from a band who had topped the charts twice in the last year and deluxe canapés which I hadn't spent hours painstakingly constructing myself?

The condoms I'd had since catering college—but never had the guts to use—were burning a hole in my jewelled clutch purse alongside the business cards. I wasn't even sure why I had popped them in there this evening, except that I'd had it drummed into me at a young age never to take a chance.

But after my weird reaction to seeing Camaro kiss the supermodel, I began to wonder. Perhaps I needed to kick-start more than just my future career prospects?

Belle had a wonderful child. An amazing career. A gorgeous billionaire who I suspected was already halfway in love with her... And she was probably having the best sex of her life right about now... While I had never even had a boyfriend.

Which surely totally explained why had I got all hot and bothered over having a sex god like Camaro lock gazes with me.

And whose fault was that, exactly?

It's your fault, Jess. For always being so terrified of taking a risk.

I'd come to Paris alone, and snuck in here tonight, with the goal of beginning a new career path for myself. But maybe rather than touting for business what I needed to do was use this opportunity to stop hiding from life.

So go for it already!

Nerves fizzed alongside the vintage bubbles. If I didn't finally manage to lose my virginity tonight, I could at least put my spectacular vintage Dior dress to good use and take a crash course in flirting 101.

I'd show Renzo Camaro. And everyone else here, I added hastily.

And the best way to do that was to make my first, and probably only, masquerade ball a night to remember.

No one here knew who I was. Which meant if I kept my newly minted business cards in my purse, I could be whoever I wanted to be tonight. Not the tomboy virgin who left her foster home at sixteen to pursue a career in catering… Not the unnoticed mousy cousin of one of the Super League's top R&D experts who needed to schmooze for business tonight. But a mysterious femme fatale in red satin.

Cinderella, hold my beer.

Renzo

Who is the girl in red?

And why the heck had she been captivating me all evening? Because the unfamiliar mix of jealously and arousal which pulsed in my gut every time I glimpsed her dancing, with a variety of increasingly unsuitable men, was driving me wild.

Something about her had reminded me vaguely of my

former R&D expert, Belle Simpson, when I had first spotted her from the balcony as I greeted the guests. But that didn't explain the need which had coursed over my skin and made me ache. Or why I felt motivated to kiss Edina in front of everyone—because I knew she was watching us.

It had been a long time since I'd needed, or wanted to make a woman jealous. And I'd certainly never had to work to attract one. Because all I usually had to do was wait for them to come to me... Just ask Edina.

And that vague similarity to Belle should be a turn-off too.

Belle had always had *unattainable* written all over her. And I had never been the kind of man who cared to sleep with women who came with strings attached. Because that sounded like far too much work.

'Renzo, why don't we sneak away to your suite, you know you want me, darling?'

I turned to find Edina pouting at me with that look in her eyes which I'm sure she thought was sultry, but I found boring. When we had hooked up over a month ago, I had told her I never slept with the same woman twice, but she had refused to get the message.

Perhaps you shouldn't have kissed her then, just to make the girl in red jealous?

I stifled the lowering thought and snagged Edina's wrist to lift her grasping fingers from my lapel.

'This is my party, Edina,' I murmured, holding onto my irritation to avoid a scene. 'So I cannot simply leave.'

'Of course, you can.' She pouted some more. 'You have your playboy reputation to protect,' she added with a teasing grin, which failed to amuse me. Especially when I caught a glimpse of the girl in red behind her.

Her lithe body gyrated to the music, her subtle curves

mesmerizing me in that damn dress which shifted and glowed, clinging to her high firm breasts like a second skin.

The shot of adrenaline careered through me unchecked. *Again*. And began to annoy me. Why was I holding back? And waiting for her to approach me? I had sensed her awareness of me when our gazes met earlier. So why not approach her? I certainly hadn't slept with her before, because she would not intrigue me now if I had.

Edina grasped my cheek again, the way she had earlier on the balcony, but my patience was at an end. I jerked my head free. And sent her a tight smile.

'You force me to be blunt, Edina,' I said. 'I told you, I have a rule I never break. Which means I have no desire to bed you again.'

She gasped at the insult, but it was clear she had got the message when she hissed, 'Why do you have to be such a bastard, Renzo?'

I laughed. 'Because that is what I was born to be,' I replied, the familiar insult one which had not bothered me in years. My wealth and success had insulated me from the brutal indignities of my childhood—which was precisely why I had worked like a dog to escape them.

Edina stormed off, but she was instantly forgotten as my gaze tracked back to the girl in red, still dancing alone on the other side of the ballroom. But then one of my reserve drivers—Jack Rogers, a young man with a promising future on the track—swung in behind her and rested one hand lightly on her hip to whisper something in her ear.

She glanced over her shoulder, startled, but then sent him a shy smile.

Fury burst in my chest—bright and brittle and incandescent—galvanizing me to storm through the crowd towards them. Rogers's bright future was about to crash and burn if he didn't take his hands off her. Because I had just decided, tonight, the girl in red would be mine...

CHAPTER TWO

Then...

Jessie

'DID THE LADY ask you to put your hands on her, Rogers?'

My head swung round at the gruff comment, to find Renzo Camaro standing in front of me, glaring at the guy behind me.

The shock to my system was swift and predictably chaotic—even though I'd been busy ignoring him all evening and concentrating on enjoying myself. But nowhere near as swift as the speed with which the hand that had been cupping my hip disappeared.

'Hey, Mr Camaro, great party,' the guy stuttered. 'I didn't know she was yours.'

'She's not!' I announced, finally finding my voice, as my outrage caught up with the ripple of awareness which had blindsided me. How dare the two of them talk about me as if I wasn't even there.

And how could Camaro look even more gorgeous when he was behaving like a caveman. And why was he?

Before I could consider either of those questions though, or get a handle on my reaction, the guy behind me was gone, scared off by his boss. Something about that bugged me even more. Was every woman here just supposed to be part of Camaro's smorgasbord of available bed partners? I could still remember in far too much detail the kiss he'd planted on the supermodel Edina Grant earlier. What had happened to her?

The music the DJ was playing shifted down a notch, into a slower and sexier R&B tune. Camaro stepped closer, his lips quirking in a wry smile as he looked at me, *really* looked at me.

My breath clogged in my lungs. Annoyingly.

Why was his attention so intoxicating? When he was behaving like a jerk? *Again*.

'What is your name?' he asked, as his bold gaze swept over my features.

I opened my mouth, to blurt it out. But then I realised, I didn't want him to know who I was. I didn't want him to put me together with the mousy tomboy who he'd never noticed before. Tonight, I had decided to be someone else… And somehow I seemed to have succeeded, because he had never looked at me before with interest in his eyes.

'Why do you want to know?' I asked provocatively, deliberately avoiding his question.

'Isn't it obvious?' he murmured, confusing me. But then he stepped even closer, so close I could see the flecks of gold in his irises, and smell the scent of luxury soap, clean man and a subtle, expensive cologne. His gaze lifted to the chignon I had spent an hour arranging, and I was suddenly aware of the sweaty tendrils which had escaped during the hours of dancing and now clung to my neck.

My cheeks heated at the thought of how dishevelled I must look.

But instead of disdain, what I saw in his eyes was approval as his gaze returned to mine. 'Why will you not tell me your name?' he asked again.

His voice was so husky it seemed to reverberate at my core. Then he lifted his hand and ran his thumb down the side of my face and over the mask. His touch was light and fleeting, but the brief contact was electric. I jolted back. He laughed at my transparent reaction, his chuckle rough with amusement, and arrogance. And more of that intoxicating approval.

Before I could come up with a plausible reply he added, 'If you have crashed this event, I have no intention of asking you to leave.'

'Good to know,' I murmured, feeling brutally exposed and wary now, as well as impossibly aroused. How had he got the upper hand so quickly? And why had the hot stone returned to throb and ache in my abdomen, when I'd spent the evening convincing myself it was a freak reaction never to be repeated?

I sent up a silent prayer of thanks for the mask—which at least afforded me some protection from that all-seeing gaze—and my weird reaction to it.

He laughed again. 'So you *are* a party crasher.'

I frowned back. 'I'm not sure what's so amusing.'

'Believe me, *Principessa*,' he said, the regal Italian title rolling off his tongue like an endearment, and disturbing me even more. Had he read my mind earlier, when our gazes connected? Did he know for one brief moment I had kidded myself I was a princess? But then he added, 'If you knew how I have been unable to take my eyes off you all evening, you would know what is so amusing...'

My heart thundered in my ears, and my ribs cinched tight around my lungs. The awareness in his eyes was so vivid now, I was breathless. And the hot stone had turned to a wave of lava again flowing down to my core.

But then I remembered the devastating kiss he'd given

another woman only a few hours ago, which had left me feeling empty and embarrassed—and I got a grip. This man was a practiced seducer, who thought he could click his fingers and any woman he wanted would come running. And even if I couldn't control the lava, I did have some pride.

'Would that include while you were sucking the face off Edina Grant?' I shot back, with a saccharine sweet smile.

'Touché!' he murmured, the husky chuckle returning. Apparently I hadn't offended him with my bitchy comment. *Well, damn.*

'You noticed that?' he asked, as if he was pleased by my reaction, not embarrassed by his shameless behaviour.

'Didn't everyone?' I replied, trying for indifference and getting disgruntled instead.

'I like that you are jealous, *Principessa*,' he countered with a total lack of remorse which should have infuriated me, but didn't, *quite*. 'This is good, because that is precisely why I went to the trouble of kissing Edina in the first place.'

'If that's supposed to be flattering, it's not,' I replied, trying really hard to ignore the idiotic dart of excitement in my chest.

Who cared if he had noticed me earlier? And why would I want him to make me jealous? When that kiss just confirmed what an arrogant, immature jackass he was?

A supremely hot arrogant immature jackass, the traitorous voice in my head whispered, turning the dart into an arrow—which threatened to deflate the last of my outrage.

'I'm sure Edina appreciates you stunt kissing her,' I managed, trying to hold on to my indignation.

'Edina will get over it. She certainly had no complaints about the quality of my stunt kiss…' he said, his confidence as annoyingly intoxicating as his arrogance.

The music changed again, to something deep and rhythmic, the bass beat throbbing, and so loud I was forced to tilt my head up to hear his reply. He took the gesture as an invitation—because, of course he did—and cradled my cheek in his callused palm.

I shivered, his touch like a lightning rod. I could hear his supreme faith in his own abilities when he whispered against my ear, 'Would you like me to demonstrate, *Principessa*?'

His hot breath turned the ripples of sensation into an earthquake of temptation, the lava into an inferno. I stared up at him, my eyes probably full of the yearning I had tried so hard to ignore all evening. I licked my bottom lip involuntarily and he swore softly.

Suddenly, I was pressed against him, his lips covering mine—firm and seeking and devastatingly demanding. I opened for him instinctively and his tongue plundered, his possession complete.

The music pounded in my heart and throbbed in every part of my body as he grasped my head to angle my mouth and take more. The partygoers around us faded away. I couldn't seem to pull away from him, couldn't seem to stop the yearning, the need which had turned the ache at my core into a dark desperate longing to be filled. To be taken.

He ripped his mouth away abruptly and swore again. His gaze was unfocused and almost as stunned as mine. Gone was the arrogance, the confidence, replaced with something that looked like the same frantic yearning I felt.

Why did that make it so much more terrifying?

He dropped his hands from my cheeks, which were burning now as I took in the crowd surrounding us, who had all stopped dancing. Some were grinning, some staring—a few were looking almost as shocked as I felt.

He grasped my hand, taking charge. 'Let us take this demonstration somewhere private,' he announced, then marched through the crowd, which parted before him like the Red Sea before Moses.

I tried to calm my racing heartbeat as I struggled to keep pace with his long strides. We left the dance floor and entered the adjacent ballroom, where I had first spotted him what felt like several lifetimes ago.

I didn't feel like that girl anymore—foolish, mortified, confused. Instead I felt energized, aroused and bolder than I had ever felt before.

Renzo Camaro hadn't just noticed me, he wanted me. And while a part of me knew this was dangerous, another part of me was eager to ride the whirlwind, to fulfil the yearning which I had struggled with earlier and which he had ignited with a simple kiss.

I chewed on my stinging lips.

Okay, not *that* simple a kiss, to be fair. More a statement of ownership. A tantalizing preview of what was to come.

We raced up one sweeping staircase and reached the balcony. He led me to a side door where a bulky man in a dark suit stood guard.

The security guard said something in rapid Italian and Renzo replied in English.

'Tell my staff not to disturb us until morning, Francesco.'

The man nodded and held open the heavy oak door, but as we stepped into a wide corridor, lit by elaborate wall sconces, the scent of fresh paint permeating the air, I found the will to dig my heels into the plush carpeting.

'Wait! Mr Camaro.'

He stopped abruptly and turned to me. 'My name is Renzo,' he said.

'I…' I gulped down the anxiety closing my throat. 'I don't remember agreeing to sleep with you,' I managed, as he continued to stare at me.

A muscle in his jaw jumped, and something flickered in his expression, which looked oddly like desperation. But surely, I had got that wrong.

Camaro had kissed a ton of women before me, and I knew I wasn't special. I was just another notch to add to his bedpost. Quite probably the second notch of this evening. But even knowing I was just one in a long line of willing women, I knew I wasn't going to refuse him. I'd never had this brutal yearning before tonight, and it seemed appropriate that I should want to have it fulfilled by him, because he'd triggered it after all. Also he had a reputation as a man who knew how to satisfy women. And it seemed like a good idea to put my first time in the hands of an expert.

But even knowing I wanted him, I wanted this, I also wanted him to at least deign to ask me properly first.

He cradled my cheek, then rubbed his thumb across my lips, which were still sore from that marauding kiss.

'Your eyes tell me that you want me, and so did your lips,' he said. But then he dropped his hand and stepped back. 'But if you wish to say no, of course you can.'

The wicked smile was mocking, but I wasn't sure who he was mocking, me or himself.

'I don't want to say no,' I was forced to admit. 'But there's something you should know…'

I hesitated. Should I tell him he was my first lover? A part of me was scared he would stop, or worse be appalled. The spurt of inadequacy from earlier began to put a big dent in my newfound confidence.

But then his eyebrow lifted and his lips quirked in that mocking smile, and I knew I couldn't lie to him.

'What is this thing I should know?' he prompted, because I was standing in front of him like a dummy.

'I… I've never done this before,' I blurted out.

Instead of looking surprised or appalled, the mocking smile remained firmly in place. 'Never done *what*, *Principessa*?' he asked, as the heat in his eyes intensified.

It was clear he really had no idea what I was talking about. My face heated so swiftly it was probably glowing in the shadowy hallway. Seriously, I was going to have to spell this out?

'You know...' I swung my hand between the two of us. 'This *thing*. Tonight.'

'What thing?' he asked again, enjoying himself, as I drowned in embarrassment. He gripped my flailing fingers and brought them to his lips. 'You have never had sex in Paris?' he teased, as he kissed my fingertips, sending the heat south. 'Perhaps you have never had sex with a man who is dedicated to making you come so hard you scream?'

He sucked my thumb into his mouth. The sensual pressure made me bite my lip to contain a groan.

'Or maybe you have never had sex with a man who does not know your name?'

The gleam in his eyes became as dangerous as it was charming and my face—and a few other key parts of my anatomy—threatened to spontaneously combust.

'There is a simple solution to this problem—take off the mask and tell me who you are, *Principessa*.'

I dragged my fingers free and rubbed my hand along the satin of my dress, my skin sizzling.

'I've never had sex with anyone before,' I replied.

His eyebrows launched up his forehead. And I could see I had actually managed to shock this unshockable man.

'You are not serious?' he said, his voice rough with disbelief. Then his gaze swept over me, the mocking grin history. 'How old are you?'

'Twenty.'

His shoulders all but slumped with relief. And he said something in Italian under his breath which sounded like a curse and had everything inside me becoming sharp and discordant.

Jess, you dope, why did you have to tell him the truth?

He was staring at me now as if I'd grown an extra head. And my embarrassment turned back to mortification. *Time to make a speedy exit.*

I turned, intending to head back to the ball and get the heck out of Dodge. I had made a fool of myself. Of course, he didn't have any interest in initiating a virgin. Why had I made a big deal about it? But before I could go far, he caught me, wrapped his arms around my midriff and brought my back flush against his hard chest to halt my getaway.

His breath was warm against my nape.

'Don't go,' he said, and for the first time, he actually sounded sincere.

But it was too late, I felt compromised and exposed. What on earth had made me think I could pull off the femme fatale act with a guy like Renzo Camaro?

'I should leave,' I said, struggling to get out of his arms. 'It's obvious you don't want to sleep with me anymore,' I added, while trying to sound indifferent, because I couldn't bear to make an even bigger fool of myself and have him pity me.

But to my surprise his arms tightened and he murmured, 'Surely even a virgin can tell when a man wants her. It is not something I can hide,' he said. 'Especially if you don't stop wriggling.'

And then I felt it, the prominent ridge nestled against my bottom. I stopped struggling, the evidence of his desire making the lava sweep back into my core.

'Oh,' I said, stupidly flattered and exhilarated—the embarrassment fading.

He turned me in his arms. There was gravity in his voice when he asked, 'Are you concerned I will hurt you? That I cannot be gentle? That I will be a brute? Because of the stories of my past?'

I was so unprepared for the question—and the wounded frustration in his expression before he could mask it—I blurted out the truth. 'No... I'm not even sure I want you to be gentle.'

I just need you to want me—with the same passion I want you.

I shoved the thought aside.

Needy, much?

'Then why did you run?' He frowned, not prepared to let it go.

It was obvious I'd offended him, and I was not sure how. His ego had seemed indestructible until now. But as the silence stretched between us and he continued to stare at me, I knew I had to tell him the truth. Or as much of the truth as I could risk without tearing what was left of my pride to shreds.

'Because I thought you didn't want to do it anymore,' I said. 'Once you knew you were my first.'

He indicated the strident erection still ruining the line of his suit. It would almost be comical if it weren't so—I swallowed heavily—so unbelievably hot.

'Well, you were wrong,' he said. 'The pants do not lie, no?'

I laughed. I wasn't sure if he was trying to be funny, but I relaxed nonetheless. 'Yes, I see your point,' I said. '*Point* being the operative word.'

'And now she makes fun of the effect she has on me,' he

declared, with mock indignation. 'I hope you know being in such a state is painful.'

'Sorry.' I sniggered, enjoying his chagrin and his discomfort if I was honest. It felt ridiculously empowering to know I was the cause.

He grasped my hand again, opened my fingers, then lifted my hand to his mouth and bit into the flesh at the base of my thumb. I jolted, the moan escaping my lips as heat flared.

'That is payback,' he said.

I nodded dumbly, not able to speak anymore, my need painful now too.

'Do you still wish me to be your first, *Principessa*?' he asked.

I nodded with embarrassing enthusiasm, stupidly touched not just by the direct question, but the rawness in his tone. And the fierce desire in his eyes.

Maybe I was just another conquest to this man. I had no doubt at all I was not the first virgin he'd slept with either. After all, if he had seemed surprised earlier, he seemed super confident again now.

But as he led me down the corridor and up a flight of stairs to his opulent living quarters, my heart thumped against my ribs. Had I made the right decision? To trust Renzo Camaro to show me what pleasure really meant? When I had never trusted any man before him? I didn't know. But for once, I refused to second-guess myself. And the lava pulsing like wildfire in my sex.

Renzo

What the hell was I doing? The girl was a virgin. And not only had I never bedded a virgin before now, I had never had any desire to bed one. I preferred my women to know exactly what they wanted, so I could give it to them. Where was the enjoyment in having sex with someone who did not know how? There could even be blood!

But as the horrifying thoughts circled in my head, I led her towards the master bedroom, gripping her hand, and I knew I couldn't let her go.

I wanted her with a passion which had only become more desperate since that damn kiss on the dance floor. More than that, I even *wanted* to be her first lover.

I *wanted* to be the man who would introduce this woman to the joys of sex. The first man to hear his name on her lips as she dissolved in ecstasy.

As soon as the shock of her revelation had worn off, instead of being turned off, I had been even more turned on. Tonight, she would be mine. And only mine. I would be able to possess her in a way no other man ever had.

I refused to question my bizarre reaction. This was surely just because she was the first woman in a very long time who had actually challenged me. I was so used to women fawning over me, and falling into my arms at the mere click of my fingers, that my sex life had become jaded without me even realising it.

Instead of finding her refusal to bow to her desire for me annoying, I had found it refreshing—and surprisingly hot—to see the spark of outrage when I had staked my claim to her. And then there was the chemistry between us, the intensity of which was not something I had experienced either in a very long time. Or possibly ever. Our kiss on the dance floor had been even more exciting and electrifying than my own first kiss in a back alley in Rome when I was a thirteen-year-old runaway.

The memory of that desperate first kiss with a woman far older than me, who had laughed at my inexperience, made my palms sweat unexpectedly as I turned the girl to face me. The red satin gleamed in the subdued lighting. Her breasts were high and firm, her breathing ragged. She stared at me with undisguised longing in her eyes.

My confidence returned in a rush. I was not that desperate boy anymore. Far from it.

But how could she be so transparent and yet also so much of an enigma?

I reached to take off her mask. I wanted to see all of her face. Wanted to know who she was.

But she grabbed my fingers to stop me. 'Don't.'

I frowned. 'Why not?' I said, the frustration making my tone brittle.

But she didn't flinch, the pensive smile which lifted her lips more enigmatic than the Mona Lisa's. 'I don't think I can go through with this if you take off the mask,' she murmured.

Once again, her honesty stunned me. I was used to women who liked to play games, who flirted and teased and enjoyed it when I flirted and teased back. Sex had always been a game to me, a chance to prove myself, to show I could conquer any woman, could make any woman I desired moan and beg… But she was different. Not just her virginity but the complete lack of subterfuge.

I dropped my hand, because I could see she meant it. That this would be over if I did not acquiesce to her request.

A part of me was frustrated. This was another new experience. I had never wanted a woman so much before that I would allow her to make demands I didn't like.

I bit my tongue, forced myself to push the easy smile back onto my lips. I refused to let her see she had rattled me. But I knew I wanted her too much not to agree.

Damn.

'Okay,' I murmured.

She shivered with relief. Why did keeping her identity a secret mean so much to her? And why did her infuriating request only captivate me more?

The need throbbing in my groin made it clear I would have to answer those questions another time.

I took off my jacket and threw it over a chair. Then loosened my tie and unbuttoned my collar.

She watched me, the arousal in her eyes flaring, along with the blush on her cheeks, which lit freckles on the bridge of her nose I noticed for the first time.

Perhaps she liked to play games after all, I decided...

The pounding in my groin intensified at the delicious thought. And some of my irritation subsided.

Fine, I happened to be an expert at these sorts of games, and I already knew she was not.

My sensual smile became genuine as I leant against the dresser and crossed my arms over my chest.

'I will make a deal with you, *Principessa*,' I said, inspired.

She nodded, the wary tension in her expression encouraging me. She might win the battle, but she would never win the war.

'What's the deal?' she asked, turning my smile into a grin.

I flicked my gaze over her. 'You can keep the mask, as long as you lose everything else.'

It was an outrageous demand, and for a tortuous moment I worried I had gone too far. After all, I would hazard a guess she had never stripped for a man before. But something about that precedent only made me want to see her strip for me even more. I waited, as the vicious need pushed my desire to fever pitch.

Was she as brave and bold as she appeared?

The blush on her face spread across her collarbone, making her pale skin almost as vivid as her dress. I could see the pulse throbbing in her neck, could feel her wariness from across the room. But I could also see the outline of her nipples as the peaks hardened, and the pale blue of her irises disappearing as her pupils darkened with lust.

Desire crackled in the air around us, as potent and provocative as anything I had ever felt. It was a major struggle for me to remain aloof, to hide my desperation when she nodded, agreeing to the deal.

I continued to wait, aware of her hesitation, but finding it as beguiling as it was frustrating. I would let her take her time, even if the anticipation killed me. I uncrossed my arms and sank my hands into my pockets as she released the pins in her hair. The fragrant mass drooped on one side, then tumbled to her shoulders. She shook her head, and the long chestnut curls bounced.

I wanted to sink my fingers into the silky mass so badly, to drag her head back and devour the throbbing pulse in her neck, to see those hard peaks and kiss them until they swelled into my mouth, I was starting to sweat. But still I waited, curling my fingers into fists, and inhaling the sweet aroma of feminine arousal like a drowning man.

Had I ever wanted a woman as much as I wanted this one? If I had, I certainly couldn't recall it. But then in that moment I seemed to have no past, no future, only the present moment, as the anticipation and need pounded through my veins.

She sucked in an unsteady breath, then located a zip under her arm and dragged it down with trembling fingers. The sound was deafening in the quiet room, the vague bass beat of the music from downstairs nothing compared to the throb of my own heartbeat.

I swallowed heavily as the bodice fell.

Dio, no bra.

I dragged in my own ragged breath as her breasts were revealed, the areolae ruched and pouting. My dry mouth flooded with moisture. The desire to suckle on her swollen flesh and make her moan became so intense it was painful.

She wriggled her hips to ease the satin down until it puddled at her feet. Then folded her arms over her breasts, making her cleavage swell.

She lifted her chin, her stance defiant. My heart pushed against my throat. She was stunning. Her boldness, her bravery somehow even more captivating than the sight of her naked flesh, soft and glowing in the lamplight. The thin swatch of lace shielding her sex and that damn mask were the only items of clothing she had left as she stepped out of her heels and kicked away the satin.

I cleared my throat. 'You missed something, *Principessa*,' I mocked, indicating her panties with a slight nod.

She shook her head. 'I'm not losing anything else until you lose something too,' she declared.

It was all the invitation I needed.

'Bene,' I said, more than ready to strip. My skin already felt too sensitive for clothing—as pheromones fired through my bloodstream.

I flung off my tie, then unbuttoned my shirt the rest of the way with frantic fingers as I crossed the room towards her. I had lost the shirt too by the time I reached her. Her head barely reached my collarbone so she was forced to tilt it back to meet my gaze.

I settled a hand on her bare hip, felt her tremble of response. The scent of her arousal intoxicated me, as her eyes widened and she took in my naked chest, her gaze burning over the crude tattoos I had had inked into my skin as a boy, the many scars which had been the cost of that same misspent youth.

My heart punched my ribs. And for one unprecedented moment I was actually nervous. What if she was disgusted by the marks which revealed the degradation of my past?

But when her gaze connected with mine again, what I saw made my breath stall in my lungs and my heart skip several beats.

Not disgust, not even the excitement women usually responded with when they saw the evidence I could not hide of the gutter rat who had existed before I had made myself into the billionaire playboy.

No, as she blinked furiously, her pale blue eyes took on a sheen of emotion. And she lifted her finger to trace the jagged scar on my cheek.

'Renzo, I'm so sorry,' she whispered.

For a heartbeat I was undone—by her sympathy, her compassion. But then my stomach twisted. How dare she pity me.

I grabbed her wrist, to drag that consoling finger from my face, determined not to be moved.

Her eyes widened, but she didn't resist.

Our chemistry might be off the charts, but this connection could only ever be about sex. If she thought she could get under my guard, she was sorely mistaken.

Holding her hand, I moved it down, to press it against the strident erection.

'Unzip me, *cara*,' I murmured, my voice raw with need. 'Before I explode.'

Jessie

I shivered as the husky demand reverberated in my chest and made my nipples tighten.

I concentrated on locating his zip, while trying to keep my breasts covered. I knew I must seem clumsy, unsure and woefully inexperienced as it took me an eternity to find the stupid tab. But he remained still, and said nothing, giving me time to calm down. After he'd had me strip, was it any wonder I was already a bundle of nerves…and my senses had melted into a pool of liquid yearning?

I tugged the tab down with infinite care, aware of the erection pressing forcefully against the fabric. Then let out a relieved breath, as I revealed black boxer briefs—the stretchy fabric distorted by the hard ridge.

Sensation rushed into my own pants and the arm I had over my breasts loosened, probably from shock, as I stared at the impressive outline.

How is that going to work?

He tucked a knuckle under my chin. His smile was warm and impossibly sensual—and self-assured.

'Do not fear, *Principessa*. It will fit,' he said, and I realised he was a mind-reader. A very well endowed mind-reader. 'If I make sure you are properly prepared,' he added. 'And I will.'

My face lit up like a Christmas tree. But I knew I wasn't scared, just impossibly turned on. And also stupidly glad now that I'd told him he was my first. Because there was a tenderness in his tone I would never have expected.

Still just sex, Jess. Don't get carried away. Of course, he wants it to be good… For both of us.

'Glad to hear it,' I said, jauntily, trying to dispel the pulse of emotion. 'Because it looks like a monster.'

His grin widened and he chuckled. 'You flatter me,' he said. 'Although, it is true, I am much bigger than the average man,' he added, clearly teasing me, although I suspected he wasn't entirely joking. Because, seriously, it looked *huge*.

But all thoughts of his size, and how on earth I was going to accommodate him, dissolved in a pool of molten need, as his thumb trailed down from my chin and skimmed over the arm I had covering my breasts.

'Let me see you,' he asked softly. My arm released automatically.

The need intensified as he stared at my naked breasts.

At last, he cupped one heavy orb, and circled the aching peak until I had to bite back a moan. I shuddered and tensed, but then—just when I thought I couldn't take any more, my breast so swollen, the nipple so tight and hard— he leant forward and licked the aching tip.

I cried out and shuddered uncontrollably, clutching his head in my hands as he went to work with that devious mouth. He used teeth and lips and tongue, focusing intently on my pleasure as the waves built, arrowing down from my breasts to between my legs. I could feel my panties becoming damp as the desire swelled and pounded.

I was panting, shuddering, shaking, when he lifted his head at last. It was only then, when his gaze locked on mine, his face taut, his eyes impossibly dark, the scar on his cheek rigid, that I realised he was as turned on as I was.

'*Sono molto sensibili?*' he asked in urgent Italian.

'I'm sorry, I don't speak Italian,' I replied.

He laughed, the sound rich but not that amused. 'Your breasts, they are very sensitive, did you know this?'

I shook my head, the fierce approval in his expression making my throat dry.

He dragged off his trousers, and the boxer shorts. I got a brief glimpse of that strident erection—which was even more magnificent than I had realised—but before I had a chance to panic, he knelt in front of me.

'*What*…what are you doing,' I asked, as I gripped his broad shoulders, my own knees so weak I could barely stand.

He gazed up at me, inhaling deeply, then grinned. 'Seeing how sensitive the rest of you is.'

Gripping my hips, he pressed his face into the apex of my thighs.

Before I had a chance to be embarrassed, at how wet I was already, he sighed and licked his lips, the smile becoming wonderfully lascivious. 'I can smell already how delicious you will taste.'

I let out a rough chuckle, which turned into a shocked groan, as with his teeth, he gripped the lacy underwear I had bought especially that morning.

The sound of ripping fabric was deafening. I jolted, digging my fingers into his shoulders—and the crudely drawn bird of prey inked on the tanned skin—as I struggled to stay upright. His hands steadied me, bracketing my hips, as he propped one of my legs over his shoulder, opening me to him completely, then dragged me towards his marauding mouth.

Before I had a chance to brace myself, his tongue delved into the swollen folds, slick now with my juices.

Delicious heat tore through me as he devoured me in devious, devastating strokes. He teased and tormented me with his tongue, until I was nothing more than a raw, pulsating nerve—desperate for more, scared it was already too much. I gasped, the pleasure so intense I couldn't breathe. I couldn't think… All I could do was feel.

'Please…' I moaned, needing more, but not sure what.

The desire spiralled and flared, the vice at my core yanking tighter and tighter until he answered my pleas, by capturing the heart of my pleasure at last and sucking hard.

I sobbed, as the vice released in a rush and pure unadulterated bliss burst inside me.

The waves crashed through me, leaving me slumped over him, my whole body glittering with afterglow.

I was unable to stand any longer, but just as my knees gave way, he stood and hefted me easily onto his shoulder.

Upside down, I could see the bulge and release of his superb glutes—the scars and tattoos that covered his back as he carried me effortlessly, like a sack of potatoes, to the bed. Before I had a chance to be embarrassed, though, he laid me down, then climbed over me, the huge erection butting against my thigh.

'Are you ready now, *Principessa*?' he asked.

It wasn't really a question—because surely he knew I would refuse him nothing, my body a throbbing mass of desperation—but even so he waited for my nod.

'Let's check,' he said, still watching my face, as his fingers delved, brushing across my clitoris.

I bucked upwards, startled by how sensitive I was. But also by the renewed yearning.

'Mmm,' he said, as he lifted his fingers to his lips and licked them. 'I will take that as a yes.'

He bracketed my hips and lifted me to probe at the swollen folds with the huge head of his erection.

I gripped his arm, to stop the thrust I knew was coming.

'I… I have condoms with me,' I managed, surprised I could think straight, let alone speak.

His head rose, and for a moment he looked as dazed as I felt, then colour slashed across his cheeks. Was he blushing?

The thought was somehow ridiculously touching as he groaned then murmured, 'Yes, of course.'

He reached across me, retrieved a condom from the bedside table and rolled it on. But his fingers weren't entirely steady, and my heart bounced erratically.

Had I undone him, as much as he had undone me?

Emotion swelled in my chest, joining the vivid joy crushing my ribs.

But then he gripped my hips again, angled my pelvis and probed for a second time.

'Hold on to me,' he said, his voice as raw as I felt. I clung to his broad shoulders, suddenly feeling vulnerable and exposed but also so desperate to have the hollow ache filled.

'You must tell me if I hurt you,' he added.

Then he was pressing into me. The thick girth felt immense, as he thrust slowly, surely.

I flinched at the pinch of pain. He stopped abruptly, sensing my distress, and his gaze locked on mine. What I saw made the hollow ache wrap around my heart.

'Too much?' he asked, his voice raw, his shoulders trembling with the effort to hold back.

I shook my head. 'No, please don't stop. I want all of you.'

He grunted, emotion flaring in his eyes as he thrust the rest of the way.

I could feel him everywhere, the pain, the soreness though was nothing to the immense swell of connection, the wrenching intimacy which seemed to echo around the room in our shared breaths, as the passion flared.

He waited, for me to adjust to his size, then pulled out, thrust back—slowly, carefully but with a ruthless purpose—until he had established a relentless rhythm which made the pleasure build again. But it felt wilder, and rawer and somehow more elemental this time. And so much more terrifying.

I gripped his shoulders, my eyes stinging, my throat raw, my heart thundering against my ribs, as the pleasure climbed—higher and higher—building from my core, searing and unstoppable.

I sobbed, I begged, not sure I could bear any more.

But he knew I could as he pushed me further still.

'You must come for me,' he said. Part seduction, part need, all demand.

The pleasure shattered, sweeping me over the crest at last. But as I tumbled freely into the abyss and heard him shout out behind me, raw emotion burst in my chest, and my stunned heart felt as if it had shattered too.

Renzo

What the hell just happened?

I tried to force my mind to engage, as I pulled out of her body, her tight flesh releasing me with difficulty. The sense of something fundamental shifting inside me was terrifying, as I stared at her flushed face. She stared back at me, her eyes dazed with afterglow, but still so sure. And unafraid.

I had never had an orgasm like it. So intense, but also so raw, so basic. The effort to hold back, to take her slowly, to be gentle had been unbearable. Was that why I had been able to feel her every breath, sense every shift in her emotions?

I rolled away from her, flopped onto my back, feeling hollowed out. And far too aware of each staggered breath she took beside me. Had she felt it too? That connection? Which I had no desire to acknowledge, because it made me feel so exposed.

I sat up, dragged myself out of the bed, even though I wanted desperately to tug her into my arms, to ensure she was okay. This too was a completely new experience—the desire to indulge an emotional connection, after the sex was done.

As I headed into the en suite bathroom, the need pooled again in my groin.

Not done? *Seriously*? How could I want her again so soon? This was madness.

I tugged off the condom, flushed it down the toilet in too much of a panic to do my usual forensic check to ensure there would be no consequences. To think I had very nearly taken her without protection... Another scary thought.

I stood over the sink. Braced my arms on the vanity. And stared at my face in the mirror.

Get ahold of yourself, Camaro.

I was still the same man, still the same playboy bastard who used women then discarded them. Great sex, even stupendous sex would never change that, I told myself staunchly.

After washing myself, I wrapped a towel around my hips and strolled back into the bedroom. But when I saw her scooping her dress off the floor, something vicious twisted in my gut.

'*Che cosa?*' I murmured, shocked. Then I remembered she didn't speak Italian. 'What are you doing?' I translated, even though a part of me had realised in that split second it would be better if I let her go now. Got her out of my life, before I broke any more of my golden rules.

She glanced over her shoulder, as she held the gown to her breasts, covering herself from my gaze... Another brutal shaft of *something* assailed me.

Was it anger, frustration, regret? Who the hell knew.

'I should go,' she said in a hoarse whisper, her expression echoing the panic I had felt moments before.

It was the last thing I had expected her to say. Shouldn't

she be making demands now? I had just taken her virginity. But somehow, because she wasn't asking for more, wasn't making an issue of it, I felt oddly deflated, and also annoyed.

Who was using whom here?

'Really? Why must you?' I asked, raising an eyebrow, determined not to reveal the fierce unknowable feeling building under my breastbone. 'Because that makes me feel a bit cheap,' I added, only half joking.

She blinked at me, clearly not sure whether or not I was teasing her. The fact that I was not sure myself increased my irritation…and the inexplicable desire to make her stay—for the rest of the night.

That I didn't want her to leave yet was another first. But I would just have to examine that urge too at a later date.

'I… I thought you'd probably want me to go now,' she said, her artless expression somehow heartbreaking. Normally she would not have been wrong… Why did that make me feel like a bastard, when it never had before?

'You thought wrong,' I said.

I walked around the bed, and placed my palm on her cheek, unable to prevent myself from touching her. I could feel the warmth of her blush. I brushed my thumb over her full bottom lip, and her tremble of response echoed in my groin.

The towel around my hips lifted and her gaze darted to the reaction I couldn't hide.

'I… I don't think I can do it again just yet,' she said with a lack of guile which only captivated me more.

I let out a rough chuckle. I didn't want to be enchanted, but how the hell could I stop myself? 'Ignore it. As I said, I have no control over my body's reaction. But I do not have to act on it.'

She nodded, and the blush flared across her collarbone,

visible above the gown she still clung to as if it could protect her from my need.

Good to know I could beguile her too, I thought wryly.

'How sore are you?' I asked, as my thumb touched the pounding pulse in her neck, surprised to realise how much her answer mattered to me.

She looked away. 'It's fine,' she said, embarrassed. 'You were very gentle.'

I knew I hadn't been as gentle as I could have been. But I felt stupidly grateful that she seemed okay.

I took her hand, to lead her into the bathroom. 'Let's get you washed up,' I said, the urge to take care of her another novel experience.

Doesn't mean anything. Just that she is your first virgin.

As the thought occurred to me, I knew I would never take another virgin, not if I could help it. Surely that was why I felt this strange sense of responsibility, this wave of protectiveness towards her. Another new experience I did not particularly like...or know how to handle.

She tugged on her hand. 'It's okay, I can do that myself when I get back to my hotel.'

I kept my grip firm on hers, before shifting round and lifting her easily onto the marble vanity unit. 'Let me,' I said, as I gently eased the gown from her hands, and handed her a towel to cover herself.

Her blush was so vivid now it was practically glowing. But she nodded.

I took my time, soaking a flannel, easing her thighs apart and wiping away the evidence of our love-making, and her lost virginity. She tensed slightly as I finished.

But as I glanced up, concerned I might have hurt her, what I saw on her face was arousal.

I tensed. The desire to tear off that damn mask, and take her again, all but overwhelming.

'Don't look at me like that, *Principessa*,' I said, the need turning my erection to iron. 'Or I may break another of my golden rules.'

'What golden rule?' she asked, as if she really didn't know.

I clasped her neck, dragged her mouth to mine, then forced myself to place a chaste kiss on her forehead. 'Don't ask.'

I flung the flannel in the laundry basket and scooped her into my arms.

She let go of the towel to cling to my neck and need fired through my body again at the sight of her breasts bared to my gaze.

But I could see the glow of emotion in her expression, so I forced myself not to join her as I placed her on the bed and covered her with the quilt.

'Go to sleep,' I said, as she stared at me, her gaze showing a depth of emotion which scared me even more than the pounding need I could not hide.

She had no idea who I really was. The things I'd done to survive, to prosper, and for the first time in a long time I was ashamed of that man.

'You're not going to join me?' she asked, her innocence all but crucifying me.

'Soon, I have a few things to do first,' I lied.

She nodded and then curled into a ball and fell instantly to sleep.

The knowledge that I had exhausted her didn't help with the need surging through my body. Not at all.

I wanted to join her, wanted to wrap myself around her… But knowing I wanted it too much made me determined not to give in to the urge. I had never needed a woman like this before… Certainly not once the sex was over.

I didn't like it. Because I had never needed anyone, relied on anyone but myself. And it made me feel vulnerable in a way I hadn't been since I was a very young child.

Concentrating on the sinking empty sensation in the pit of my stomach I remembered from my childhood, I forced myself to leave her lying on my bed and walked from the room.

I took a long hot shower to wash off her scent in one of the guest suites. But as I dried myself, somehow I could still smell her intoxicating aroma.

I considered returning to the ball. I even flirted with the idea of seducing someone else to help me forget what had just happened. But even as the thought occurred to me, the hollow ache twisted inside me and I knew no other woman would be able to fulfil this need tonight.

I realised I had no desire to even look at another woman, because all I really wished to do was return to my own bedroom and discover the identity of the woman in my bed. To hold her, to see the need in her eyes, to make her want me again.

The thought horrified me, because it suggested a need for approval, for validation I hadn't yearned for since I was too young to protect myself—or my mother—from the disgust of others.

I was not that pathetic child anymore, though.

Refusing to acknowledge the bitter emotions raging inside me, I dressed swiftly and took the back staircase to the underground garage.

I send a text to my housekeeping staff, informing them of the woman in my bed and how to handle her when she woke up in the morning. But as I climbed into my favourite sports car, and drove through the streets of Paris, away from her, I couldn't seem to escape the brutal, pointless yearning I thought I had let go of long ago.

She was the cause. Whoever the hell she was. I knew this. Which meant I must force myself to forget her.

CHAPTER THREE

Then...

Jessie

I WOKE SUDDENLY from the forceful erotic dream, impossibly turned on... I blinked, aware of every place where my body felt pleasantly achy, even a little sore.

Sunlight shone through the ornate shutters on the floor to ceiling windows of the palatial bedroom. The expensive linen sheets felt like gossamer against my skin.

Renzo Camaro's bedroom. Where I had spent the wildest, most exquisite—and exquisitely disturbing—night of my life.

I stretched, the familiar heat firing over my skin.
Wow.

Recalling the sex was bad enough, but then I remembered the way he had insisted on taking care of me afterwards, and tucking me into his bed, with a gruff tenderness which had made my heart ache as well as every other part of my well-used body.

The man's reputation as a lover was clearly well earned. But what had surprised me was that his reputation as a playboy, a user of women seemed less so. I had been prepared to leave as soon as he left the room, but he had seemed not just surprised but almost hurt by my attempt to flee.

I eased out of the bed, glad he wasn't lying beside me.

I felt so awkward now. And also a bit raw emotionally. I knew I shouldn't read too much into last night. It had only been a hook-up. No promises were made, and however inexperienced I was when it came to sex, I had always been aware that physical intimacy had no connection to emotional commitment. I had seen my mother discarded too many times to count, and been forced to pick up the pieces often enough, when the men she clung to walked away from her.

Plus however spectacular the sex had felt to me, it was probably nothing out of the ordinary for Renzo.

I headed to the bathroom and—after figuring out the array of intimidating knobs on the walk-in shower—let the jets caress my skin, aware of all the places where I felt strange and new.

Well, you certainly found out what all the fuss is about, Jess.

Forced to put on the gown from last night, and throw the remnants of my panties in the bin, I felt hopelessly self-conscious—*hello, walk of shame*—as I left the bedroom in search of my host.

I was eager to see him now, and yet also nervous. Aware that my heart was feeling tender too after last night, even though it shouldn't. I wasn't wearing the mask anymore. The whole idea of keeping my identity secret from him seemed ridiculous now, the antics of a silly virgin.

Don't beat yourself up too much—you were a silly virgin.

I was still arguing with myself, and blushing profusely, when I turned a corner, and bumped into an older woman, dressed in black, carrying a tray laden with breakfast items.

Luckily, she was more alert than I was and managed to rescue the tray.

'I'm so sorry,' I said, absolutely mortified. She had to be

Renzo's housekeeper. Was she wondering what the heck I was doing here?

But when she smiled, she didn't seem surprised.

'*Bonjour, mademoiselle.* I have breakfast for you, on Monsieur Camaro's orders.'

'Oh.' My stomach twisted, at the realisation that finding strange women in Renzo's apartment in the morning was perfectly normal for her.

I was just one of many, I knew that, but having it made so clear to me made my stomach hurt. My gaze skated over the tray—flaky croissants, an array of exotic fruit, something under a silver hood that smelt almost as delicious as the scent of freshly brewed coffee. But I had never felt less hungry in my entire life.

'Where is Monsieur Camaro?' I asked, before I could stop myself.

The woman smiled again, but this time it was tinged with pity.

'He has returned to his estate in Cap Ferrat, *mademoiselle*, early this morning.'

What? Really?

'Oh, right, I see,' I mumbled, trying to sound upbeat and as if I knew he wouldn't be there.

But even though I had been expecting the brush-off, had steeled myself for such an eventuality, I was still shocked he hadn't even stuck around long enough to say goodbye. Or to find out who I was.

Because he doesn't care—now he's bedded you, he's finished with you.

'He says, you may stay here as long as you wish. Myself and the rest of the staff are at your disposal,' she added gently. 'He asked for me to purchase you clothes so you may leave with dignity,' she finished, horrifying me even more.

Seriously? He had arranged to have my torn panties replaced? The mortification engulfed me, right alongside that miserable feeling of being a burden which had marred so much of my childhood.

I nodded, suddenly desperate to get away as soon as possible. But she insisted on leading me to a guest suite, where an array of expensive designer clothes, all in my exact size, awaited me—including what I suspected was extremely pricey underwear.

I actually wanted to die. But I forced myself to wait until she left. I slipped on a pair of the plainest panties I could find—deciding it was okay to replace the underwear he'd torn—but I didn't take anything else. The vague sense he was paying me for sex—possibly even for my virginity—made the grinding pain in my stomach worse.

I wanted to hate him, as I rushed out of the back entrance of the palatial residence, and returned to my hotel. But the hate I wanted to feel—the hate that might cover the aching pain of his summary rejection—wouldn't come.

I spent the next week in Paris in a daze, going over every single second of our interaction in minute detail.

When I returned to Nice, it was obvious that something serious was going on between Belle and Alexis, so I decided not to burden my cousin with the tawdry tale of my one blissful night in Renzo Camaro's arms.

A month later, I discovered the foolish aching pain in my heart—and the empty space in my gut—wasn't the only thing Camaro had left me with.

I didn't think of him as Renzo anymore, after all he didn't even know my name.

I returned to London, unable to confide in Belle about my pregnancy—which didn't even seem real. How could this have happened? I forced myself to contact his office.

Forced myself not to feel embarrassed. I was going to have his child. And he had a right to know.

I wasn't the only one responsible after all.

But my attempts to make contact with him failed. I cursed my stupid decision not to tell him my name. But after a while I began to sense it was not the fact I couldn't identify myself—or had to be so cryptic while communicating with a series of his many assistants—that was stopping him from returning my calls.

My suspicions were confirmed when I received a single text from his executive assistant, ten long weeks after our one night together.

Monsieur Camaro has asked me to wire you five thousand euro and request that you do not attempt to contact him again.

I was shell-shocked, dazed by the callousness of the text. He didn't know I was pregnant, because I hadn't told any of the many people I had spoken to while trying to reach him in person. But even so, it was clear he had decided I was some kind of gold-digger. The thought sickened and humiliated me—and made me feel like my mother, a woman I had always sworn I would never emulate.

A woman who had clung to men, who had searched desperately for love in all the wrong places because she needed their validation, because she had no self-esteem of her own.

I was resolved to have the baby. *My* baby. Alone. And never to contact him again—after replying to his executive declining his financial offer.

But three days after that text, while I was working a double shift in my new job in a kitchen in a hotel in Mayfair, trying to save the money to launch my catering business,

CHAPTER FOUR

Four years later
Now...

Jessie

'ACTUALLY, I ASKED you here under false pretences, Jess.' Belle beamed at me.

The guilty flush on her face made her look even more beautiful as she nursed the latest addition to the Galanti clan while we sat on the terrace of Villa Galanti, the stunningly beautiful Belle Epoque mansion where Belle had grown up as the daughter of the housekeeper, and which she had managed to turn into a home in the four years since she had finally married Alexi.

I grinned back at her, trying to ignore the tug in my heart as I watched her newborn son, Gaspar, sucking voraciously on her nipple. Her three-year-old twin daughters, Sofia and Isabel, were playing nearby with the gifts I had brought from London.

It was embarrassing to realise this was the first time I'd come to visit Belle here since my fateful night in Paris. I was actually quite annoyed with myself.

The family had invited me to Monaco many times, but I'd always struggled at the thought of seeing Belle with the bleeding started. Within twenty-four hours, the baby I thought would be mine—and mine alone—died inside me.

I was devastated. Hollowed out.

Alone and in pain, I contacted Belle and she rushed to my bedside. I didn't tell her that I'd had a miscarriage. Because I couldn't.

I felt like a fool. Heartbroken and empty. But a small part of me was also relieved.

Not because I hadn't wanted my baby. But because I wasn't sure I had wanted it for the right reasons. Had I wanted it because it was my child? Or because it was his?

And finally, as I began the long slow process of repairing my body, and my stupidly naive and romantic heart, the empty ache inside me finally turned to the hate I had wanted to feel for the man who had made me feel so much, but had never felt anything for me in return.

her children in her home—even Cai, their oldest son who was now eight years old and who I had always been close to because I had helped to bring him up before Belle and Alexi reconciled.

Just another layover from my disastrous night with Renzo Camaro, I realised.

It was way past time I moved on from that night. I'd been burying myself in the work I loved in the last four years, establishing my business and a stellar reputation as a personal events chef. My list of clientele was growing and I had made a name for myself in the sort of circles in which Belle and Alexi moved, helped immensely by Belle's insistence on singing my praises to anyone who would listen.

And it was not as if I needed to worry about meeting Renzo. I knew he had had a crash fourteen months ago on the track. And had disappeared from the social whirl since.

He had even sold the Destiny Team.

Not that I'd been keeping track of him, I told myself.

Then why are you thinking about him?

'Well, whatever your ulterior motive is, I'm glad to finally be here.' I smiled back at Belle, determined to stop thinking about him. 'And meeting this little one is an added bonus.' I stroked the baby's head, the feel of his downy hair and the smell of baby powder turning the tug in my heart into a definite yank.

I ignored it. There was no reason I couldn't have a family of my own. Eventually. Now my business was thriving. Just because I hadn't found a man I felt comfortable dating yet, surely I would soon.

'He's wonderful, Belle. Just like all your kids.' I grinned, glancing at the girls, who were starting to squabble over their new toys.

Belle laughed, her expression full of the frustration of

motherhood. 'Hmm, I think we can reserve judgement on that. I'm fairly certain Cai for one would not agree with you about his—' she lifted one hand to add air quotes '—far too many sisters.'

I laughed, feeling lighter than I had since I had made the decision to visit her in Monaco at last.

'So, what's the ulterior motive?' I prompted.

'It's more of a massive favour,' she said, looking sheepish. And now I was intrigued.

But I knew, whatever it was, I'd do it. I felt guilty for being so absent in Belle's life for the last four years. And for never having the guts to tell her the truth about what had happened in Paris.

We had been as close as sisters once. And the distance between us—which she had tried to bridge for years—was all my doing. I needed to repair our relationship.

She lifted the sleeping baby off her breast, and handed him to me, while repairing her clothing. She took him back almost instantly, but even so I felt the pang in my chest.

For goodness sake, Jess. Get over yourself.

I could see she had noticed, but she didn't say anything. She took a moment, rubbing the baby's back to burp him, before looking at me directly.

'I don't know if you remember him, but before Alexi came back into my life, I worked for a guy called Renzo Camaro.'

Even though I'd been thinking about him, the mention of Renzo's name gave me such a shock I couldn't disguise my reaction. I tensed, while blushing profusely.

Belle sent me a soft smile. 'Apparently you do remember him?'

Does she know? Somehow?

For a moment I was terrified.

But then she added, 'He was kind of unforgettable, especially where women were concerned.'

The tension in my gut eased, a bit. She thought I was just another woman who had noticed the infamous playboy's many charms.

'I remember he was always flirting with you,' I said, trying to keep the bitterness out of my tone. My anger had nothing to do with Belle—and everything to do with my inability to fully process Renzo's casual rejection all those years ago.

It was never meant to be more than a one-night hook-up. You have to get things into perspective.

'Renzo flirted with everyone...' Belle's smile became pensive. *'Once.'*

I was confused—why were we talking about him? Especially as I really didn't want to talk about him.

'I heard he had an accident and sold his team,' I said, suddenly curious. Even though I didn't want to be. I had stopped scouring the press and the celebrity media for information about him years ago, at the suggestion of the therapist I had seen for a while after my miscarriage. But it occurred to me, I hadn't seen anything at all about him in over a year.

'Yes, he did sell Destiny. In fact, he sold it to Alexi,' she said.

I was kind of surprised. Alexi and Renzo had always been fierce rivals. But I tramped down on my curiosity. Renzo's life was nothing to do with me, and never had been.

'Alexi must have been pleased,' I said dismissively, hating the foolish yearning to find out more about him.

'Actually, Alexi wasn't. Not really. And neither was I,' Belle said.

'But wasn't Destiny his main rival?' I asked, even though I didn't know much about the Super League.

'It was, and Alexi and Renzo were never friends, but we could both see the reasons for him selling to Galanti were all wrong.'

'I don't understand.'

'The crash… It changed him.' Belle sighed, and I felt a strange ache in my chest.

'I thought it wasn't that bad,' I said, my pulse accelerating. I had broken my embargo on reading about Renzo when the crash had happened, because it had been kind of unavoidable. But I realised now there had been very few details. All the papers had said—before they moved on to another juicy celebrity story—was that Renzo had survived and would recover.

'Renzo's management team were determined to give that impression. Basically to ensure the stock in the company didn't take too much of a hit. But it was actually much more severe than they let on. He was trapped in the car for three hours. His left leg was badly crushed. And although they managed to save it, he'll never be able to walk again without a limp.' She took a moment to place the baby in his basinet on the terrace, then shouted a word of warning to her daughters. I could see the sheen of distress in her eyes, when her gaze met mine, though. And it echoed in my heart.

Camaro had been a good employer to Belle, and a good friend to her when she needed one—it was one of his few saving graces.

But I steeled myself against the squeeze in my ribs. I had no claim on this man, and no stake in his life. I had never even really known him, in anything other than a physical sense. We had had one night, the consequences of which had hurt me deeply, and which he had refused to acknowledge. But ultimately, those consequences were gone now. A part of my past that I needed to keep in my past.

But even so, I couldn't stop myself from murmuring, 'That's tough for someone who used to be so active.'

'It's not just the physical trauma that's the problem, though,' she offered, her distress palpable now. 'He's become a shadow of his former self. The crash and its aftermath have fundamentally changed his personality.'

'What do you mean?' I asked, as my ribs started to ache. Because for the first time in a long time, I was allowing myself to remember the other side of that night. The man who had initiated me with such care and attention. Who had made my first—and only—time so special. I'd convinced myself since, that had all been part of his act and his huge ego, his desire to prove himself with women, and had nothing to do with me personally. But even so I could picture his face far too clearly, an image I had suppressed for so long—the intense concentration in his expression, the flare of fierce need which had matched my own, as he had pushed me to orgasm.

'Ever since he left the hospital,' Belle continued, unaware of the turmoil of emotions I had spent four years learning to suppress, 'he's been holed up at his place in Cap Ferrat. He doesn't socialise anymore, doesn't see or speak to virtually anyone. And according to his business manager he is refusing to do the rehabilitation he needs to get as much mobility back as he can. Most of his staff have left, because he's such a nightmare to work for now. He also isn't eating...' She paused. 'He's lost a ton of weight. Which is where you come in...'

'What? *How?*' I asked.

'Henri, his manager, asked me if I could find someone to cook for him. Henri's desperate to find someone who can entice him to eat again.' She let out a laugh, but there was no humour in it. 'Renzo was always a bon vivant. And

Henri thinks he's become so depressed he's not interested in food. They've tried everything. But he won't speak to the therapists or the doctors anymore, and Henri's now desperate enough to try anything. He thinks if he can make Renzo want to eat again, he might turn a corner. He might start to want to live again too.' Her cheeks heated. 'Which was why I told Henri all about you—and your glittering credentials as a woman whose food is like manna from Heaven.'

'I'm flattered,' I managed, even though my stomach was hurting. And my heart was pounding so hard in my throat it was choking me.

I didn't want to see Renzo Camaro again. I'd spent four years doing the work to forget him. But how could I tell Belle any of that. When I'd never even told her that I had once spent a night with him? That he was the man who had taken my virginity?

'Would you do it, Jess?' She grasped my hand, her eyes full of concern. 'I know you're taking a well-earned break at the moment. And that you don't have any new commissions till the autumn. I know it's a big ask. I also know it won't be easy. Because Renzo won't want you there.'

'But surely he could just fire me then?' I said, frantically trying to think of a way out, without disappointing Belle, or having to admit to her what I had hid from her for four years.

I knew she would have been nothing but supportive. But I also knew she'd be devastated—that I hadn't confided in her. And weirdly, I also didn't want to screw up her friendship with Camaro, because it didn't sound as if he had many people left who cared about him.

'Actually, he can't,' Belle said, squashing the hope I could get out of this predicament on a technicality. 'Henri has had power of attorney on all Destiny Inc.'s holdings since the crash and Renzo's been too despondent to change that. So Henri can hire you and Renzo can't fire you.'

'But what even makes you think it will work?' I threw back at her, my ribs now feeling as if they were in a vice. 'It sounds like cod psychology to me. If he's depressed, getting him to eat a couple of great meals isn't going to change that.'

'I know it's not going to be that simple. But what he really needs is a friend, Jess. Someone who will stand up to him. Who won't let him avoid the real issues any longer. I'd do it myself but—' she glanced at the baby '—I can't leave the kids.' She cleared her throat. 'I know you don't know him,' she rushed on. 'But I also know how you went to bat for me and Cai, when I needed you. When you were still just a kid yourself. You've been on your own for a while and you've managed to overcome your own demons, by sheer strength of will.'

'What demons?' I asked. How did she know any of this?

'Your useless mum for starters,' Belle offered. Then she looked me straight in the eye. 'And the miscarriage.'

I blinked, stunned. 'You knew?'

She nodded. 'I saw it on your notes when I came to see you in hospital in London. When you didn't tell me yourself, I wanted to respect your privacy.' She shook her head, a tear leaking out of her eye, which she brushed away with an impatient fist. 'I'm so sorry you never felt you could tell me about it, Jess.'

The guilt in her expression almost crucified me. 'I should have told you, that's not on you, Belle. Good god.'

'But that's why you didn't want to come visit us, isn't it? Why you found it so hard to be around my kids?'

I shook my head, the watery smile that split my lips making me realise how much I'd missed Belle, and the strength of our connection. 'Not anymore,' I said simply.

I'd always mourn the lost pregnancy. But I should never have kept the truth from her... Or at least not that much of the truth. Telling her now who the father was seemed somehow gauche. And insignificant.

She nodded back, her answering smile full of compassion and love. 'I'm so so happy to hear you say that.'

But then she leant forward and said. 'So can you help us try and fix Renzo, the way you once helped to fix me?'

I hadn't fixed her, I wanted to say. She had made a brilliant life for herself because of her own bravery and hard work. But weirdly a part of me realised taking on this challenge—however it turned out—might actually be good for me.

My sadness, my heartache, the pain which had held me back from moving on with my personal life for so long, had never really been about Renzo. He had just been a catalyst. Surely, it was way past time I stopped running from that night? And this might be the best way to finally put that part of my past behind me.

If I could do Belle a favour at the same time, why not?

Renzo meant nothing to me, he never really had. He had just been an accidental sperm donor. So why on earth would I be so worried about seeing him again?

In actual fact, seeing him as he was now—'a shadow of his former self'—could only help to put my own suffering into perspective.

After all, Renzo was no longer living the charmed life he once had. Everyone had problems that they had to overcome, even him. I wasn't sure I could help him do that, but there could be no harm in trying. For Belle's sake.

So, before I could second-guess myself, I went with my gut. 'Okay, I'll give it my best shot. But don't blame me if it doesn't work.'

Belle looked elated. The tight feeling around my ribs eased a little, but, annoyingly, I could still feel that aching pain around my heart.

CHAPTER FIVE

Jessie

A WEEK LATER, I bade goodbye to Belle and Alexi and their family in Monaco and Alexi's chauffeur drove me to the Camaro estate in Cap Ferrat.

Henri Deschanel, the Destiny Inc. CEO and Renzo's business manager, was supposed to be meeting me at the estate. But when the huge metal gates of the complex opened to admit us for the half-mile drive to the villa itself, which sat on a secluded spit of land overlooking the clear blue waters of the Mediterranean, I asked the driver to let me out.

I only had a rucksack with me—I'd always enjoyed travelling light—and I wanted to clear my head before I arrived.

As soon as I began the walk, though, I saw the signs of neglect, in the overgrown pine forest which covered the estate and made it seem so cut off from the rest of the neighbourhood. Given that Cap Ferrat was such an exclusive area, and the real estate so expensive, most of the chateaux here were built close together within carefully manicured grounds. But Renzo's home was very different: the acres of trees cut out the light, until the driveway opened to reveal a four-storey Belle Epoque chateau, as grand and ornate as the Galantis'. But unlike Belle and Alexi's home, the Camaro *palacio* was marred by neglect, its paintwork peeling and the circular flower beds which surrounded the huge eighteenth-century structure dry and filled with weeds.

I could see the edges of the cliffs beyond the chateau, which led down to the boat dock, the pool house and the private beaches the estate had once been famous for...back in the heyday of Destiny's success—when Renzo had been famous for throwing lavish parties at a moment's notice, which would be splashed all over the celebrity press.

But now the house and its grounds were eerily quiet, the ghosts of Renzo Camaro's high society lifestyle evident in the broken marble tiles, the heliport beside the overgrown lawn which didn't look as if it has been used in months. It was almost as if Renzo's home was under a spell, a cruel enchantment which had destroyed his once glittering billionaire lifestyle.

I swallowed down the fanciful—and stupidly sentimental—thought as a middle-aged man appeared from the grand oak doors of the chateau.

He jogged down the circular stone steps to greet me, looking debonair but informal in jeans and a light sweater.

'Mademoiselle Burton, I did not realise you were on foot, or I would have driven out to collect you,' he said in perfect if heavily accented English.

'It's okay,' I said as I shook his hand. 'I fancied the walk.'

'I am Henri—we spoke on the phone,' he added.

'I know,' I said, surprised to realise Destiny Inc.'s CEO appeared to be a little nervous.

He nodded. 'I must apologise first of all for the state of the Camaro *palacio*,' he said, glancing at the dilapidated estate. 'Every time I have hired new staff, ever since Renzo returned from the hospital, he has made their lives so impossible, they have refused to stay.' He huffed, looking embarrassed now, as well as harassed. And I began to realise why he looked so concerned. He was expecting me to go the same way as all the others. Was that why he had insisted on paying me a small fortune to do this job?

'What exactly are you expecting of me?' I asked. Because all the contract had mentioned was cooking Renzo regular meals and maintaining the kitchen area. 'I'm not really trained to do more than cook.' Was he expecting me to do the gardening too? Or worse, become involved in Renzo's care?

'Oh yes, yes, I know,' he added. 'We have a cleaning crew who come in twice a week but who cannot enter his room—and another new grounds crew who start tomorrow.'

'What about Mr Camaro?' I forced myself to ask. 'Exactly how much interaction am I expected to have with him?'

Belle had talked about me becoming his friend. That was not going to happen. But I was not equipped to become his carer either.

'All you need to do is bring him the meals. And take them away again. He no longer needs nursing care. Although he's not that mobile.' He cleared his throat, looking uncomfortable. 'He never leaves his suite. But I must warn you, he's angry still about his injury. And he takes that anger out on the staff. He's not violent. I would never...' He stared at me, his cheeks heating. 'I would never put an employee in that situation. But I apologise ahead of time for anything he might say to upset you. Believe me, his temper is not really directed at you, but at himself.'

I nodded, beginning to see the scale of the problem.

'You don't need to apologise,' I said. 'After all, you're not responsible for his behaviour—he is.'

The poor guy looked so relieved, I realised how tough the last fourteen months must have been for him too.

'Belle said you are a strong woman. But if at any time you wish to terminate our contract, I will understand.'

'Okay,' I said, suddenly determined not to do that.

I was here now, and I wanted to see this through. Maybe I wouldn't be able to help Renzo Camaro, but I was prepared to try.

Of course, he might be even less inclined to have me here if he recognised me. But I doubted he would. Not only had I worn a mask through our entire encounter, but I had long ago accepted I was just one of the many women he had had in his life. And his bed. He had probably already been sleeping with someone else by the time I had woken up that morning, alone and pregnant in his bed.

I allowed the small spurt of resentment—and sadness—to fold around my ribs. And fire my determination.

It was already obvious, before I had even met him again, that Renzo didn't need people around him who were going to indulge his temper tantrums. Or get sentimental about who he used to be. The good news was, however tough this was going to be on me, it would be tougher on him, because he wasn't that man anymore. And it seemed he knew it.

I settled into the small housekeeper's cottage at the edge of the gardens, just below the pool. Then spent some time in the kitchen, sorting out the groceries I had ordered in. Thank goodness, the large catering space was well equipped and scrupulously clean. But it was beyond weird that once Henri left later that afternoon, I was alone in the huge empty chateau, with Renzo. For a man who had once been surrounded by people, it seemed inconceivable he had become a virtual recluse.

Henri had given me a list of Renzo's favourite dishes. I'd also taken advice from his doctor, who had suggested I avoid any foods which were too rich, given the small amount he had been digesting of late. So, I got to work making fresh linguine with lobster in a light tomato sauce in the palatial kitchen as the afternoon edged towards evening.

Kneading and proving the dough for some ciabatta rolls, as well as going through the painstaking process of making the pasta, helped to calm the tangle of nerves in my stomach. But it bothered me to realise how nervous I still was, an hour later, as I climbed the staircase to Renzo's suite of rooms in the East Wing with his supper.

I knocked sharply on the door. Silence. I knocked twice more, but there was still no response. Renzo knew I was here, he was expecting me, Henri had confirmed as much before he left. I knew he had to be in there, because I hadn't heard any movement in the house while I worked.

The nerves in my stomach tangled into a tight knot.

Terrific.

For one brief moment, I considered leaving him to stew for tonight. And eating the dinner I'd prepared myself.

That's the coward's way out, Jess. You agreed to take this job, so you could finally put that night into perspective. Seeing him again is all part of the process.

I cleared my throat. And called out.

'Mr Camaro, it's Jessie Burton, your new chef. I've got your supper. Shall I bring it in?'

'Je n'ai pas faim!' The shout was raw and rusty, the tone full of animosity, but even so the sound of his voice—the fluent French flavoured with his Italian accent—had a shiver rippling down my spine. And triggered the aching pain in my abdomen…

The tray shook in my hands, and I wondered if I had made a massive mistake coming here. It took every molecule of courage I possessed to ignore his shout, push open the door with my backside and walk into the room.

The sitting room of the suite smelled musty, the furniture barely visible in the shadows. The room was much cooler than the rest of the house. I could see the door was open leading into his bedroom, but heavy drapes cut out the light from the stunning sunset I had noticed from the terrace.

I forced myself to cross the sitting room. I tapped on the open bedroom door with my foot then walked in.

'I said I am not hungry. Do you not understand French?' The gruff shout from the bed startled me, but I didn't look round, the knot of nerves in my stomach rising into my throat.

'Yup, I understood. But I've made it now, so I might as well leave it here in case you get hungry later,' I said briskly, as I marched across the dusty carpet, placed the tray on the dresser beside the balcony doors.

Determined not to be cowed by his attitude, I threw open the drapes and forced open the doors onto a large terrace.

Light streamed into the room, covering the dark wood furniture with a golden haze—but the blast of evening air did little to dispel the scent of despair and hopelessness which hung in the air.

A vicious curse made me swing round. And my gaze landed on the man in the bed—highlighted by the setting sun.

I bit into my lip to hold on to the shocked gasp which wanted to burst out of my mouth.

I had expected Renzo to look different. But I hadn't expected him to look completely unrecognisable.

The once effortlessly charming and expertly groomed seducer—whose beautiful face and hard lean physique had been able to make any woman sigh—glared at me out of a gaunt sallow face covered in a thick beard. His hair was long and unkempt, his movements laboured and clumsy as he pushed himself up in the bed. The sheet—which from the smell now reaching me I suspected hadn't been changed in weeks—fell to his waist, revealing the sunken lines of his once magnificent torso. The scars and tattoos I could still remember in far too much detail stretched over the defined ridges of his ribs.

The tangle of nerves was joined by an unwanted surge of horror... And pity.

He looked as if he hadn't eaten properly in months. And the tight muscle flexing in his cheek suggested he was in some discomfort, a pain which wasn't just caused by my unexpected presence in his room.

'Get the hell out of my bedroom,' he rasped.

I nodded, determined not to react to the surly tone, and the stupid pulse of sympathy.

'I'll be back to pick up the tray in the morning,' I said, because for some stupid reason I didn't want him to get the last word.

I was hightailing it out of there, though, the tangle of nerves threatening to strangle me, when he growled. '*Arrête* Who are you? Do I know you?'

I was so shocked, I turned towards him. He was still glaring at me, but now his fierce gaze roamed over my face. My heart galloped into my throat as the familiar sadness coalesced into a ball of misery in my stomach.

'I'm Jessie Burton. Belle's cousin,' I murmured. 'We met, a long time ago, when she worked for you,' I added evasively.

It wasn't a lie, but it was also a long way from the whole truth.

Most of me hoped desperately he didn't recognise me from our night together. Because that would get awkward, fast. But as he continued to stare at me, a darting pain in my chest told another story. And I realised to my horror there was a small part of me that wanted him to recognise me. If only to validate that one night, and the consequences which I had borne in my body for a few agonising weeks.

Seconds ticked by as my face began to burn, the dark emerald green of his irises fired with something I recognised too, not arousal but fierce awareness. My skin prickled alarmingly, and I hated myself for responding to him. Even now.

I also hated that small part of me which was still that hopeful, romantic girl who needed this man's validation—who could still seek his approval even after he had discarded me so easily.

But then he broke eye contact, covered his face with his arm and flopped back on the bed.

'Just get out,' he groaned, the despair in his voice somehow calling to that stupid girl too.

I ruthlessly ignored the dart of sympathy and disappointment as I closed the door firmly behind me.

CHAPTER SIX

Renzo

Was it her? I wondered, as the echo of something stirred in my groin which I hadn't felt in years.

The high cheekbones, the heart-shaped face, the full lips, the sprinkle of freckles across her nose. And those pale blue eyes—so deep, so wary—as they watched me had all seemed familiar, probably because that girl had haunted my dreams for four years...

But how could it be her? The girl whose virginity I had taken what felt like a lifetime ago—when I had been another man, living another life? The girl I hadn't been able to forget, even though I had wanted to? The girl who had tried to contact me and who I had ruthlessly discarded.

My mind, my body had to be playing tricks on me. Casting me into a new level of hell. As if I wasn't in a deep enough purgatory already.

It isn't her. Even you cannot deserve such torture.

Ever since they had prised my shattered body out of the mangled wreckage of the Destiny prototype, and cast me adrift in a new horrifying reality, I'd been a stranger to myself. A man who was only half-alive, and half-whole and who could no longer hide from the truth of who he really was.

A failure. A fraud. Not the billionaire playboy, but the gutter rat who had done anything and everything to get out, to get away from the squalor of where he had started.

I dropped my hand from my eyes, to gaze out at the redolent orange and gold of the sunset that my new—and unwanted—employee had revealed so cavalierly.

I kept the drapes closed for a reason. I hated to look at myself, to see what I had become. So I lived in darkness again. The way I often had as a young runaway. Feral and starving and desperate to escape his guilt and his destiny.

To think I had thought I had once outrun my fate and named the racing team I loved Destiny to make it official. A grim smile twisted my lips at another unwanted irony.

With the terrazzo doors open, though, the salty breeze began to freshen the sour smell in the room, and the dying sunlight warmed my skin.

I lay there for what felt like forever taking in the novel—and not entirely unwanted—sensations. But then a whiff of something delicious filled my nostrils—garlic and oil, tomato and… Was that lobster? My nostrils flared, and my stomach growled in protest.

I stared at the tray she had left on the chest of drawers beside my bed. And scowled.

But my stomach, dormant for so long, continued to protest. I was furious that it was tempting me out of my stupor. But I couldn't seem to prevent myself from crawling out of the bed, despite the angry protests of my withered leg, and the unused muscles that cramped as I rose.

I threw off the coverlet, using every ounce of the strength I still possessed to stand, determined to throw the damn tray off the balcony. I wobbled precariously, clasping the bedpost, angered even more by the weakness and exhaustion that dragged at me, as I staggered, each step sending shards of agony through my leg, the torn ligaments stiff and painful.

After five agonising steps, I finally reached the chest, my naked body dripping with sweat, the effort to stay upright so great I was panting like a man who had run a marathon not simply crossed a room.

Ashamed of my weakness, I glared at the damn tray, grasping the wooden beading on the chest to stay upright. It took all of my remaining strength to lift the silver dome covering the food. But when I did, the determination to throw away the meal I didn't want was whisked away on a tantalising breath, as the intoxicating aroma consumed me.

The freshly made pasta was covered with a light tomato sauce which gleamed in the sunset, the succulent chunks of lobster—once a favourite indulgence—tempting me beyond reason.

My hollow stomach howled, begging me to take a bite.

I stood there, shaking and sweating, naked and pathetic, staring down at the perfect dish for what seemed like an eternity. Unable to throw it away, but also unable to take that small incremental step away from the misery I had wallowed in for so long.

Eventually, I could not withstand the temptation any longer. I lifted the fork in trembling fingers, wound one long ribbon of pasta around it. Scooping up a bite of lobster too, I shoved the food into my mouth. The flavours burst like sunlight on my tongue. Rich and fresh and sensual—the perfectly spiced dish sent visceral pleasure through my system for the first time in over a year. A low moan escaped my lips and I shovelled a whole mouthful in next. I ate too fast, gulping down one mouthful then another—like a starving man—and was reminded of those rare occasions when I had had the chance to eat my fill as a boy.

But after only a few forkfuls, I had to stop eating, my empty stomach rebelling at having to digest too much, too fast.

I stood, still shaking with pain and effort. My gaze tracked to the horizon, through the open terrazzo doors. The pure blue water of the Mediterranean darkened as the sun dipped, casting an eerie light over the estate I had once been so proud of.

And for the first time since I had locked myself in my suite, I noticed the overgrown flower beds which I had refused to allow anyone to tend, the pool below my bedroom, which I had demanded be emptied, and was now strewn with leaves.

And then I saw her. The woman who had brought up my meal. The girl I had mistaken for *her*.

She was walking towards the housekeeper's cottage, which sat below the pool terrace.

I scowled, the throbbing pain in my thigh, the cramping indigestion in my stomach replaced by the swift shock of *something* again as I watched her lithe, economical movements.

I staggered to the bed, and crashed back onto it, as angry now as I had ever been, not just with my injury, my weak and useless body, but also with her.

Whoever the hell she was, and however good a chef she was, I did not want her here—making me even more aware of everything I had lost.

And as soon as she returned to pick up the tray tomorrow, I would tell her so.

At least, that was what I had intended, until my stomach relaxed, and the unfamiliar feeling of fullness softened the soreness in my limbs, and dragged me down into the deep well of sleep.

Jessie

I woke early after a fitful night, disturbed by so many dreams, in which the past and the present had merged and Renzo's gaunt form still possessed the commanding presence of the man I remembered.

Even as I stared at the overgrown grounds from the safety of the housekeeper's cottage, the strange sensations found in dreams continued to streak through my body...sensations which had been dormant for years, but still had the power to scare me.

How could Renzo Camaro as he was now—broken and weak in both body and soul—still be able to reawaken the passion I had found in his arms?

I didn't want to be that girl again. I didn't want those sexual urges, that reckless desire, because it would give him the power to destroy me again. What if helping him to get stronger, turned him back into that man?

I huffed. And forced myself out of bed. As I showered, I gave myself a good talking to.

Stop overdramatising, Jess. Renzo Camaro is a broken man. He can't hurt you now. All he can do is hurt himself.

As I headed past the pool terrace to the chateau's kitchens to prepare Renzo's breakfast, I noticed the empty pool. The sun was hot this morning and I imagined how nice it would be if I could take a morning swim before work.

The new grounds crew Henri had hired in a last-ditch attempt to make Renzo see reason was due to arrive in an hour.

Henri had given me a list of things he hoped I could get Renzo to agree to, once I'd fed him properly. I checked through the list as I made up a batter for American waffles—another of Renzo's former favourite meals, incongruously—and sliced some fresh fruit to increase his vitamin intake.

I decided to concentrate on the first two items on Henri's list.

1. *Try to stop him scaring off the new grounds crew.*

2. *If you can get him to agree to see the physiotherapist, I will give you a five-thousand-euro bonus on the spot!*

Having a focus should stop me fixating on the pointless memories when I saw my new boss again.

Even so, my palms were sweating—and those wayward sensations from my dreams skittered over my skin—as I carried the breakfast tray up the stairs twenty minutes later.

I forced myself to focus on my mission—stop him being a bastard to me and his other employees, and get some much-needed physio—as I gave his door a brisk knock, then walked into the room.

To my surprise, the curtains and doors I had opened the night before were still spread wide, and sunlight streamed into the room. Even more surprising, I noticed the room smelled less fetid, a balmy sea breeze scenting the air.

'Good morning, Mr Camaro,' I announced as I placed the breakfast tray onto the dresser.

Last night's offering was still there. My heart clutched when I saw that most of the food had been left congealing on the plate, but at least a few mouthfuls had been eaten.

Success, of a sort.

'Henri wanted me to let you know the new grounds crew arrive today,' I said as I picked up last night's tray. 'I thought I'd ask them to refill the pool, so I can take a dip in the mornings before I start work,' I added provocatively, when I got no reply.

Surely goading him would at least get a response.

But when the silence continued, I forced myself to look towards the bed, then almost dropped the tray.

The bed was empty. I searched the rest of the room, then rushed to the en suite bathroom, but he wasn't in there either.

What the actual.? Where had he gone?

'Mr Camaro?' I asked, my heart ramming my throat as I raced back into the bedroom, still carting the tray. Surely, he was in no condition to go for a morning stroll? He had barely been able to sit up when I'd brought him his meal last night.

Jessie, you idiot, you annoyed him so much he ran away. Even though he can barely walk.

Just as I was becoming frantic—imagining his emaciated body at the bottom of one of the cliffs, or lying frozen after spending a night lost in the grounds—a shadow crossed the empty room. I swung round to see a dark silhouette in the terrace doorway. His tall frame was propped against the door, his sweatpants—the only thing he wore—hung off his narrow hips, but somehow his chest looked less sunken. His gaze was fierce—and a great deal more lucid than it had been the night before—when he turned into the light.

'Oh, thank goodness. You're here,' I blurted out, my relief making the tray rattle.

'Where else would I be?' he asked, his voice gruff with irritation but somehow less sulky and self-pitying.

'Good point,' I murmured, feeling the flush of awareness as my gaze absorbed the hard lines of his chest and it occurred to me that although he was way too thin, he looked stronger and more imposing than he had last night too. My gaze skated over the tattoos and scars which I had once found so compelling. The spike of awareness made me realise that hadn't changed.

Great.

I could see the effort it was taking for him to stand up-right, though, from the slight tremor in his legs, to the sheen of sweat which made his skin glow. He winced, as he headed back onto the terrace. I followed him to the doorway, and watched as he made slow, painful progress towards the chaise longue which he must have been sitting in when I arrived.

But just as he reached it, he stumbled. His face contorted as he gripped the back of the chair to stop from falling.

I dumped the tray on the dresser and rushed onto the ter-race. But as I reached out to offer him my hand, he flinched.

'Don't,' he snapped.

I withdrew my hand. And watched—emotion squeez-ing my ribs—as he braced his arms, his knuckles whiten-ing, and forced himself to put weight back on his injured leg. It seemed to take an eternity as he breathed through the pain. But when he finally managed to manoeuvre him-self around the chair, and collapsed back into it, admiration swept through me.

'You know, that would get a lot easier if you would see the physiotherapist Henri has hired for you,' I murmured, trying to sound dispassionate, as I ticked off item two on Henri's list.

'If I wanted your opinion, I would ask for it,' he snarled. The sulky tone was back.

In a weird way I was glad—it helped to slow my frantic heartbeat. When he was being a self-absorbed jerk, it was easier not to feel too much sympathy for him.

I returned to the bedroom to retrieve the breakfast tray. I placed it on the wrought iron table in front of him and whisked off the domed cover with a theatrical flourish.

'I made waffles.' I announced, mimicking the talking

donkey in a children's cartoon Belle's son Cai had made me watch about a hundred times.

Renzo's gaze shifted from the view across the cliffs and locked on mine. A surly brow rose up his forehead. Apparently, he was not an aficionado of classic kids' cartoons, because he did not look amused.

'Did I say I wanted breakfast?' he said, through gritted teeth as he shifted in the chair trying to ease his leg.

I placed the dome on the table. And straightened. I could play this one of two ways, I decided. Either I could admit I could see how much he was suffering and take pity on him...or I could play devil's advocate.

My heart was still pounding frantically in my throat—making me very aware I was not as unaffected by his suffering as I wanted to be. But I could tell from that surly scowl, the last thing he wanted, or needed, was my pity.

So, I placed my hands on my hips and let my gaze sweep derisively over his chest—which no longer looked quite as unimpressive as I wanted it to.

'You may not want breakfast, big guy. But it's fairly obvious you need to eat. Unless of course you would rather feel sorry for yourself before you finally manage to starve yourself to death.'

His brows shot up his forehead. And I could see my stroppy response had shocked him. I braced myself, ready to get the boot, less than twenty-four hours after being hired.

But then to my utter astonishment the sharp glower on his face lifted and a strangled sound came out of his mouth.

Leaning forward, he gripped his ribs and his shoulders began to shake, the strangled, choking sounds starting to alarm me... Until I realised, he wasn't dying... He was laughing. The deep, rough sound echoing across the empty estate was raw and rusty and painful, almost as if he hadn't laughed in a very long time and was relearning how.

But when he finally flopped back in the chair, scrubbing away the moisture from his eyes with his fist, and gulping for breath, the raucous laughs had subsided into low chuckles, and the tension in my own shoulders had relaxed.

When he turned towards me, though, the tension cinched tight again, darting deep into my abdomen, as I spotted a twinkle in the deep emerald of his irises I remembered. I realised his handsome face, despite the heavy beard, and the gaunt hollows in his cheeks, was no less captivating than it had been four years ago.

The shiver of unwanted sensation I had woken up with went into overdrive.

'It's lucky you are a good cook,' he said, his voice husky with the approval that had once made me do stupid things. 'Because your mouth is...' His gaze dipped. 'Very bad,' he added.

I chewed on my bottom lip, trying to contain the punch of lust as the memory of our kiss on the dance floor bombarded me and the sensation centred on my mouth.

His gaze lifted to mine. For one terrible moment, I thought he had remembered that incendiary kiss too. But then the twinkle in his eyes died, his gaze becoming shuttered and wary. The scowl returned as he looked back towards the sea.

'Leave the breakfast,' he said, his tone dismissive. 'And tell the grounds staff to refill the pool,' he added, closing his eyes, as if he was absorbing the feel of the early-morning sun warming his sallow skin—and deliberately shutting me out. He lifted his hand, doing a flicking motion with his fingers, as if I was a troublesome fly. 'I will have my lunch at noon. Now go.'

I wanted to tell him where he could stick his rude commands, but the shimmer was still there—distracting and disturbing me. So I decided to let him stew for now.

But just as I reached the balcony door and lifted last night's dinner tray from the dresser he added, 'By the way, I do not permit the staff to swim in the pool.'

I ignored the spark of anger at the contemptuous comment, aware he was deliberately trying to put me in my place. I bit down hard on my lip and swallowed down my response as I left the room.

We'll just see about that, Mr Grumpy.

CHAPTER SEVEN

One week later...

Renzo

A WEEK AFTER my new—and unwanted—personal chef had arrived I was tired and out of sorts. Each morning, I struggled out of bed before she appeared, forced myself to shower, and dress, then went to sit on the terrace, trying to look nonchalant, so she wouldn't find me lying flat on my back in the bed like an invalid. But the process wasn't getting any easier. My leg cramped painfully for hours afterwards and every other muscle in my body continued to protest at the unwanted exertion.

But worse, as I endured the pain each morning, each lunchtime and each evening, I was aware I was becoming fascinated with the annoying, insolent woman—who did not behave like any other person I had ever employed.

As I sat exhausted on the terrace this evening and waited for her last appearance of the day with my supper tray, my leg in agony from the marching I had done around and around the room this afternoon to relieve the cramping, my traitorous heart was going into overdrive in my chest. All because I was about to see her again.

How pathetic.

I heard the door to the suite open and close, and her soft

footsteps in the bedroom, and my heart crammed into my throat.

'Hello, Mr Camaro. I've made you a delicious aubergine Parmigiana for dinner tonight,' she announced as she plopped the tray on the wrought iron table in front of me. The bright breezy tone made my irritation flare. 'With freshly baked ciabatta rolls and a tiramisu for dessert.'

My taste buds were already dancing a jig as she uncovered the feast she had prepared for me. But as my gaze devoured her lean frame—disguised in the baggy T-shirt and scuffed jeans she always wore, and I noticed the flushed dewy skin of her face devoid of make-up as she straightened and grinned at me—the swell of something hot and fluid blossomed in my groin. *Again.*

The irritation twisted into resentment in my gut.

Somehow, the housekeeper I didn't even like had begun to captivate me. I was actually beginning to look forward to seeing her each day, anticipating her arrival like a love-sick teenager.

'I wanted meat tonight,' I stated belligerently, the ache in my leg now joined by the pointless ache in my groin. 'I'm sick of always eating vegetables,' I added, knowing that my anger had nothing to do with her choice of menu and everything to do with the fact I could not act on my attraction to her, even if I had wanted to. Which of course I did not, I added to myself swiftly, to stave off the familiar feeling of inadequacy and hopelessness.

I did not sleep with my employees. Even ones that fascinated and—*damn it*—aroused me.

She stared back at me, the beguiling sparkle of achievement in her face fading. For a moment, I thought I could see the soft sheen of pity—which I hated even more than my inability to even contemplate seducing her, or any other woman—but then she propped a bunched fist on her hip and her brows flattened.

'Stop being such a grump, Camaro,' she snapped, as usual not backing down for a second. Why did that only fascinate and excite me more? *Damn her.* 'Who climbed up your bum today?'

'Perhaps if you were in constant pain, you'd know who climbed up there,' I snarled, infuriated now, not just by my growing dependence on her, but how reduced I felt in her present.

'You wouldn't be in constant pain if you'd agree to work with the physio, so whose fault is that exactly?' she announced, then swept off the terrace and disappeared.

The witch.

'Come back here,' I shouted after her, only to hear the door to my suite slam.

I tried to rise, to follow her, to have it out with her, to finally get some of the frustration—at her provocative, prickly behaviour—off my chest. But sweat popped out on my brow, my arms wobbled alarmingly and as soon as I put weight on my aching leg, it buckled. I flopped back into the chair, in a sweaty heap of smashed pride, furious frustration and searing agony.

I yelled out my fury into the sultry twilight as I lay like a beached whale, unable to move.

Humiliated, embarrassed and still with that brutal swell of arousal pulsing in my pants.

I ignored it until it subsided. But as I rubbed my leg, my fingers probing the torn, scarred flesh under the sweatpants, nothing could ease my agony. Or my frustration... With her, with my situation, but—as my breathing began to even out—most of all with myself.

I had decided not to see the physio, because I knew I

could never get back what I had lost. The doctors and surgeons had told me as much before I had finally got out of the hospital…

But as my shouts faded away on the crisp sea breeze, my gaze roamed over the estate and the fury, and agony, began to fade, turning instead into something that felt like purpose.

I shovelled in the food she had brought—which was of course delicious, with or without meat, the woman had the skills of an angel in the kitchen. But as I ate, I noticed the improvements the grounds crew had made over the past week not just to the pool—the clean blue water now glittering red in the sunset—but also to the flower beds which surrounded the lawn, and the newly repaired heliport.

In many ways, the sight gave me no pleasure. Because I was reminded of why I had wanted it left. I couldn't use the pool. I couldn't even leave my room under my own steam. And seeing the estate brought back to its former glory—and the heliport operational again—only reminded me of my former life, the guests I had once had flown in from all over the globe, the endless weekend house parties and all-night raves I had loved to host, so I could scare away the ghosts from my past…

But those ghosts had been haunting me since the crash, I acknowledged. In the nightmares which crept into my dreams and echoed in my consciousness during the endless, empty days spent alone in my suite.

Except when I was thinking of or bickering with her.

As I finally found the strength to stagger back to my bed, my pride and my leg still smarting, it occurred to me that however annoying her presence, and her refusal to bow to my authority—not to mention the spark of attraction I could not act upon—I had begun to feel a little less useless, a bit more of a man, in the past week. That despite the endless pain in my leg, and the effort it took to get out of bed and shower each day, eating her food and getting the chance to snipe and snarl at her was as distracting and invigorating as it was infuriating.

When I reached the bed, I grabbed the phone on the bed-side table I had barely used in months and typed out a text to Henri.

Send physio tomorrow.

I threw the phone away and collapsed onto my bed, still angry but also resolved.

So what if I could not get back what I lost?

I didn't want to wallow in my pain any longer, because what I wanted much more was to show Jessie Burton—even if I could never again be the man I once was—I would no longer be the object of her pity.

CHAPTER EIGHT

Four weeks later...

Jessie

Whatever you're doing, don't stop. Renzo has turned a corner, the physio says he's making excellent progress. So thank you. I have just deposited another thousand-euro bonus into your account. Keep up the good work. Henri

I WIPED MY flour-dusted hands on the tea towel I had tucked into my jeans as I read the text from Henri that had pinged onto my phone.

Surprise came first, swiftly followed by guilt.

If Renzo had turned a corner in the last month, I doubted it was down to me. The man ignored me now, whenever I happened to find him in his room, which wasn't often, as he spent so much time in the specially equipped gym downstairs.

Oddly I had missed our verbal sparring. Those arguments had made me feel emboldened, empowered and seen. Pathetic really, that I seemed to want him to notice me still. But I had come to realise in the past month, I had never been more to him than another employee.

I was stupidly pleased, though, to see him leave his room each day, to work with the physiotherapist. I knew he was working hard to get some mobility back into his leg and strengthen the muscles and ligaments which had been damaged.

Perhaps I had helped to goad him into contacting the physio. But I didn't take any real credit for that. Surely even he wasn't so stubborn he wouldn't have realised eventually he needed to work on his recovery.

What I had taken pride in, though, was how much he continued to enjoy my food. But Henri was already paying me far too generously for that.

I finished cleaning my hands and texted a quick reply.

Thank you, Henri, although I'm not sure I've earned such a generous bonus. Renzo barely even talks to me.

I shoved the phone back into my pocket and started kneading the dough again. The phone vibrated against my hip. I managed to ignore it, until I'd placed the dough into a covered bowl to rise. Henri's reply, though, only confused me.

Believe me, you've earned it. You've made a big impression on him. Not only has he not asked me to fire you, he has asked me to extend your contract indefinitely.

I felt the jolt of excitement at the offer. Then felt foolish.

I couldn't stay. Even though I hardly saw Renzo now, he still had a powerful effect on me. And hearing the grunts and groans coming from the gym whenever I passed by the door to the downstairs area on my way to the kitchens shouldn't have pleased me either.

But they did.

I'd come here to make peace with what happened between us all those years ago... And instead I was becoming stupidly invested in Renzo's recovery.

And that wasn't good. For me or him.

What had begun to bother me most of all, though, was that I still responded to him, not just on a physical level but also on an emotional one. And I wasn't sure anymore which was worse. All very good reasons not to extend my contract past the end of this week.

My work here was done. Renzo was eating again, he was regaining his strength. He had also become less of a recluse, and the estate was being returned to its former glory.

I wasn't here alone with Renzo anymore during the day, and that felt good too. Or at least it should. Why on earth would I miss those early days, when it had been just me and him, constantly bickering with each other?

Of course, it was still just the two of us in the evenings. Because the other employees left each day at six o'clock. But I made a point of taking him his evening meal early and never entering his bedroom now, so I didn't disturb him—or me—after his workout...

I did still take midnight swims in his pool occasionally or in the private cove below the estate. But my act of defiance felt foolish and self-absorbed these days, because I was sure he had no idea—I suspected he was in bed most evenings long before midnight, because of the exhausting physio work.

I texted Henri a reply, even as my heart pushed into my throat at the thought of leaving the chateau in two days' time.

I have another job starting in a couple of weeks. But I'll find someone else who can come in and cook for Renzo. And I'll brief them on the menu I've created.

It wasn't true. I didn't have another job lined up for two months, but I knew that hollow feeling in my stomach was a bad sign. I couldn't risk becoming any more invested in Renzo's recovery. Because it was starting to feel personal. And the more he ignored me, the more I seemed to yearn for his attention. Also not good.

I pressed my hand to my stomach, remembering the life which had been there so briefly. Maybe if I hadn't miscarried, I would have had a tangible reason to remain here, to care what happened to him, to feel pleased whenever he devoured one of my dishes, or proud when the physio updated me on his progress while grabbing something to eat between their sessions.

But that reason had died long ago.

Henri texted a few more times, offering increasingly ridiculous sums of money to tempt me to change my mind.

Finally, I switched off the phone, because I was running late and if this was going to be one of the last meals I cooked for Renzo, I wanted it to be perfect.

I shoved the personal thought to one side, as I finished laying out the meal of seared scallops, dauphinoise potatoes and tender-stem broccoli in chilli oil and Parmesan.

The last of the staff had already clocked off when I finally carried the prepared tray up the wide sweeping staircase to his room. Nerves assailed me as I walked into the sitting area. But just as I placed the tray on the table where I usually left it now, someone cleared their throat.

My head jerked around. I straightened, the nerves intensified by the jolt of déjà vu. Renzo stood in the bedroom doorway, silhouetted against the evening sun. His hair was damp and swept back, but the heavy beard he had worn the last time I had seen him, weeks ago now, was gone.

He wore the familiar sweatpants, which hung off his lean hips. But nothing else.

My gaze leapt from his chest—no longer hollow or gaunt—and landed on his face. Heat exploded in my cheeks.

Had he caught me checking him out?

Clean-shaven, his lean face was even more striking. And reminiscent of the man who had once seduced me. I could see the changes so clearly now, from when I had first arrived. Gone was the surly scowl, the sallow complexion, the dark shadows under his eyes. He used a walking stick now, but he was standing much taller, and his face was no longer tight with pain.

I cleared my own throat, because he was staring at me, silently, his gaze intense and assessing, and it was doing nothing to prevent the heat swelling at my core and making my nipples peak painfully under my T-shirt—or the pulse of emotion in my chest. I steeled myself against the disturbing reaction.

'If there's nothing else, I'll leave this here until morning, Mr Camaro,' I said, trying to re-establish the professional distance I'd abandoned as soon as I had first encountered him here, weeks ago now.

But after the long hiatus, somehow being in his suite this evening felt so much more intimate... And dangerous. Because he wasn't the surly, broken man I had encountered then. I sensed the vitality, the intensity, the physical alertness I remembered from so long ago, despite his damaged leg.

He walked into the room, favouring his bad leg, but moving with a lot more of the grace I remembered.

'Yes, there is something else,' he said, those emerald eyes sparkling in the dying light. 'Henri says you have not accepted the contract extension.'

I nodded.

'Why not?'

'Because I have another booking,' I mumbled, hating the way the need flared in my chest, at the thought he actually cared.

'And yet we both know that is a lie. You are not booked again until September fifteenth.'

'How do you know that?' I blurted out, startled to discover he had checked my schedule.

'So you do not deny it?' he shot back, neatly avoiding the question as he caught me in the lie.

'No, I guess not,' I snapped back, angry with myself.

Why had I lied? I was entitled to leave his employment whenever I wanted now our contract was finished. 'Your supper is getting cold,' I said, then turned to leave, intending to escape before this got any more awkward.

'Don't go,' he murmured.

I stopped, shocked by the deep rumble in his tone—as if the words had been wrenched from him.

I swung round, lost for words.

'I wish for you to stay,' he said. I could see the struggle on his face. How hard it was for him, not just to admit a weakness, but to ask for my help. He inclined his head towards the tray I had left. 'Your food, it is the best I have ever tasted. It brought back my appetite when I thought nothing would.'

I was taken aback, not just by the unsolicited praise, but by the way it made me feel. I knew I was an excellent chef, and I already knew he had been devouring my food, but there was something in his voice that suggested we weren't just talking about my cooking.

I pushed the thought to one side.

Keep it professional, Jess.

'I'm glad,' I said, because I was. I didn't need his approval, but surely there was nothing wrong with accepting his praise.

'You will sign the contract extension then?' he asked. His tone made it sound like a command, but then he added, 'Please.'

The word seemed incongruous on his hard lips. But it was the hooded look in his eyes—the expression on his face—that crucified me.

Something about the whisper of vulnerability and defensiveness, so unlike the man I had met all those years ago, gave me pause...

Would it really be so bad? Could I stay for another month? Watch him heal all the way? Surely once he had become the jaded playboy again, this lingering sense of connection would finally die?

But as my mind raced, trying to justify why I wanted so badly to say yes to him, the wayward sensations—reckless, unstoppable—continued to riot over my skin.

'I'll think about it,' I said.

Even as I dashed out of the room, not waiting for his reply, though, I knew my mind was made up. That it hurt to think of leaving him told me I had to go. I had come here to confront my past, but confronting my feelings for Renzo—and those reckless sensations—terrified me, because they were all mixed up in our present now as well as our past.

Which would have been sad, if it weren't so pathetic.

CHAPTER NINE

The following night...

Renzo

'WHAT DO YOU MEAN, she hasn't signed the contract? She told me she would think about it,' I shouted down the phone at Henri, becoming frantic.

She couldn't leave. I didn't want her to leave. Not yet. I wasn't ready. I had all but begged her to stay yesterday evening. What more did she want from me?

'I'm sorry, Renzo. She told me today she is still planning to go tomorrow morning. But don't worry, she has lined up a replacement chef for you.'

'Dio!' I slammed down the phone.

No, this wasn't happening. I wouldn't let it.

I had been avoiding her for weeks now, as I worked to get my strength back.

The irony was, I had known in the last few weeks, she had been avoiding me too.

But even without seeing her every day, even without our invigorating arguments, I had been acutely aware of her presence in the house—every time I devoured her food, every time I caught a glimpse of her on the estate, every time I crashed into bed each night and dreamt of her instead of my demons.

Knowing she was here had energised and incentivised me.

The work to repair my mobility had been exhausting and time-consuming and a great deal harder than I had expected. The relentless exercise regime had been nothing short of agonising, but the physiotherapist's conviction I could get a lot more movement back had fired my determination to push through.

That and the visceral yearning which had been there all along, ever since she had first walked into my room. The yearning which had gone into overdrive last night when I had caught her in my suite again for the first time in weeks.

I limped out onto the terrazzo, the hunger pounding back to life all over again. A hunger which had only become stronger the more we avoided each other. A hunger which I had come to realise in the past month had tapered off for other women, long before I smashed up the Destiny proto-type on the Barcelona track over a year ago now. Could it be, the hunger I felt for Jessie might actually be about much more than just my recovery?

The awareness made me shiver despite the warm evening. The hazy memories of another woman…a young woman… whose virginity I had taken what felt like a lifetime ago shimmered on the edges of my consciousness, again.

The other women I had taken to my bed since that night— casual encounters which I had always found wanting—had never been as exciting, or exhilarating, as her.

Until now.

I frowned in the moonlight.

Stop thinking about that girl.

I recalled I had mixed that girl up with Jessie before, when she had first arrived. But I knew now that had been a nasty little joke fate had played on me just to mess me up even more.

But even so, I felt like Jessie had to be the key. And if I could make her stay, I could somehow figure it out.

As I struggled to unlock my brain and worked on a plan to ensure she signed the contract, I noticed the lights flicker on below the pool. It was nearly midnight, way past my usual bedtime, but the full moon glowed, illuminating the slim figure making their way along the path towards the private cove, where I had once thrown lavish parties.

Who could be swimming now?

But then the figure—dressed in a one-piece swimsuit of black spandex and holding a towel—stopped for a moment under the lamp which lit the steps down to the cove.

Jessie. Except...

The feral blast of memory streaked through my body and made the hot blood flow south. My mind reverberated with shock.

I recognised those high firm breasts—which had once been cradled in red satin—and the long slender legs, which had been wrapped around my hips as I drove into the tight wet clasp of her body.

Jessie, but also that girl.

I jolted upright, the shock of recognition doing nothing to halt the vicious spike of arousal feeding the hunger which had been building for weeks. The hunger I had been struggling to explain or contain ever since she had arrived.

I flinched as my leg protested at the sudden movement. But as I watched her disappear into the moonlit shadows, all the other things which had intrigued, and provoked me about her—ever since she had appeared five weeks ago—raced through my mind now faster than the Destiny prototype I had destroyed. And suddenly all those jagged misshapen pieces snapped sharply into place.

Why that masked girl had once reminded me vaguely of

Belle Simpson. Because that girl had been Belle's cousin. Why my reaction to my new chef's abrasive personality had fired my libido in the same way that girl's snarky challenges had once done too. Because Jessie Burton and that girl were one and the same. Just as I had sensed when I had first laid eyes on her—but forced myself to discard, because I had assumed I was losing my mind.

Shock was followed by anger, even as the vicious hunger refused to die.

Why was she here? And why hadn't she told me who she really was? That we hadn't just met as casual acquaintances because of her connection to Belle? That we had once shared the most mind-blowing sexual experience I had ever had in my life? One I had not been able to forget even though I had tried…

I shook, my hands trembling, my head starting to hurt, my leg—the muscles still sore from my workout today—cramping for the first time in weeks.

Was she here for revenge? Or because she pitied me and who I had become? Maybe she had come here intending to reignite that passion, only to find me broken and pathetic. And now she had no need of me? Which would explain why she had refused to extend the contract?

Each thought was more humiliating than the last.

But one thing I did know. She had deceived me. Lied to me. For weeks.

I stomped through the suite, tugged on a T-shirt, then grabbed the condoms which had been lying in my bedside table for over a year now. As I made my way down the stairs and through the empty house, the cramp in my leg began to ease. Even as the hunger and fury continued to charge through my bloodstream.

As my walking stick scraped softly against the stone

tiles of the pathway, the adrenaline rushed through me and I thanked god for the work I'd done in the past month.

Maybe I wasn't whole, but I was whole enough. And I was more than ready to act now on the awareness I had seen in her eyes when she had entered my suite last night, and her gaze had burnt over my naked chest.

Why hadn't I recognised that expression from long ago? Not just awareness, but compassion.

My lips twisted as I evened out my breathing. The scent of rosemary and oregano from the kitchen garden flavoured the sea air and reminded me forcefully of the food she had cooked for me. Always perfectly flavoured to make me ravenous. Now I resented that too.

The moonlight lingered on the bay, while the energy—which I had felt on the rare occasions when I had encountered her around the house in the past month—surged under my skin.

I took the narrow path through the palm trees. At last, I reached the steps down to the cove. I discarded the walking stick, it was merely a tool now, to make my limp less pronounced, but I no longer required it to stand upright... Leaning on the rail, I took the steep steps down. My thigh muscles were sore, but not painful, the sea breeze cooling my heated skin. As I reached the sand, I could hear her soft splashes which were music to my ears.

Sultry, seductive, exhilarating, compelling music, which made heat pool in my abdomen. But now I was not confused by it, just furious at her deception.

It didn't take me long to spot her in the water.

Ignoring the lounger, where she had left her towel, I propped my shoulder against the rock walls that guarded the cove and rubbed my leg absently.

But the ache there was nothing compared to the vicious

pounding in my groin as she appeared like a nymph from the dark sea. The moonlight shone on her downturned face, the line of freckles which had intrigued me once, tantalised me all over again.

The jolt of recognition fired through me again made even more heady by the sight of her full breasts, perfectly cupped by black spandex.

I had not succumbed to madness. It was definitely her. And had been all along.

The plain swimsuit should have looked unappealing—it was a far cry from the designer bikinis most women on the Côte d'Azur wore. But somehow the simplicity of her costume only made it more alluring, clinging to her slender frame and accentuating every subtle curve, every sleek muscle.

My breath backed up in my lungs.

She was as breathtaking as I remembered her. But how could the air of innocence still cling to her, when I now knew she had lied to me for over a month? And hidden her identity from me, the same way she had that night.

But as I watched her walk across the sand towards the towel, still unaware of my presence, it occurred to me finding out why she was here, why she had deceived me for so long, wasn't the only reason I had come to the cove tonight. Was that why I had snatched up the condoms on my way out of the room?

Vicious need pooled in my groin.

All I knew in that moment was that I wanted her still. She had been mine once, and only mine, and I had thrown her away—carelessly, casually—but there had never been anything casual about the sexual connection we had shared.

I would not throw it away so easily again.

I had been scared then, of the strength of that reaction.

But after everything I'd been through since that night, I knew I could handle the hunger now, to get what I wanted.

Was that why I had been so desperate to get her to sign the new contract? Why I had become so frantic? Because she had always represented my chance to become fully whole again?

Getting my sex life back was something I still wanted, desperately. And however lowering it was to admit it, she was the only woman who had stirred my libido since the crash. Indeed, since years before the crash.

I stood transfixed as she leant down to gather up her towel. She began to strip off the costume, easing the straps off her shoulders. I shifted, pushing myself away from the rock to alert her to my presence.

Her head lifted. And her startled gaze locked with mine.

'Renzo!' she yelped. 'I mean, Mr... Mr Camaro,' she stumbled over the words, and I could sense the vivid blush firing over her skin. The same heated reaction which had captivated me four years before.

The passion flared anew, thickening the erection in my pants and burning away the last of my caution.

'You should call me Renzo.' I let my gaze roam over her lush figure, brutally aware of the shudder of awareness streaking through her as she clasped the towel to her breasts. 'After all, it is way past time you stopped pretending.'

'Stopped pretending what?' she asked, as if she really didn't know.

My teeth clenched to contain the spurt of outrage. Did she still believe she could deceive me? When she stood all but naked before me?

I forced an indulgent smile to my lips, trying to be the charming playboy I had made myself become, despite the hunger and anger streaking through my body, which reminded me far too forcefully of the feral boy who had once been so desperate for the merest sign of affection.

'You can stop pretending I was not your first lover, *Principessa.*'

Jessie

He knows!

'How long have you known?' I blurted out, shivering violently.

I tried to keep the panic out of my voice. Part of me wanted to deny the truth, but another part of me was stupidly pleased he had recognised me at last. That would be the part of me that was an idiot.

'Long enough.' Renzo smiled, but the gleam in his eyes was both possessive and furious, and I knew he wasn't amused. 'Why didn't you tell me who you were when you arrived here?' he demanded, temper sharpening his tone.

I wrapped the towel around my shoulders, covering myself from that searing gaze—which skated over my figure with a sense of entitlement which was both disturbing and dangerously exhilarating. As I clasped the towel over my breasts, I could do nothing to stop the vicious shiver of reaction.

I gave a jerky shrug, trying to look unconcerned about having been caught in my lie as tension coiled in my gut.

'I didn't think you'd remember me,' I said—which wasn't entirely a lie. He had certainly forgotten me soon enough after that night. And it had taken over a month for him to recognise me again.

Even so, I hated the resentment in my tone. I despised myself for caring enough to be upset.

Humiliated, I forced myself to step past him, intending

to head back to my villa and pack my bags. But his hand shot out, with startling speed, and he snagged my wrist in an iron grip. He was standing unaided, I realised, his stance strong, and I could feel the adrenaline, the vitality pumping through him. This was not the man I had met at the beginning of the summer. But nor was he the entitled playboy I remembered either, the fierce fury in his gaze something I had never seen before.

'Where are you going?' he demanded—the pretence of humour gone.

'To pack,' I said, attempting to tug my arm out of his grasp. 'I'm leaving tomorrow,' I added, just in case he had forgotten.

'You're not leaving,' he said, tightening his grip. 'I don't want you to go.'

Something burst in my chest, something that felt almost like joy, and I hated myself even more.

Good grief, Jess, exactly how pathetic are you?

'I can't stay,' I replied, even though that stupid, needy part of me still didn't want to leave… What was that even about? 'Certainly not now.'

'Why not?' he demanded. 'Because now I know who you are?' His gaze skated over me again, entitled, provocative and fierce with challenge.

He tugged me towards him, until I was standing close enough to smell him—the tantalising aroma of soap and man. His jaw was stubbled, his hair unkempt, his clothes the usual combo of sweatpants and loose T-shirt he now lived in. His body was leaner than it used to be, but his skin was healthily tanned, those pure green eyes alive with vitality and purpose, and his shoulders were strong and broad again and his frame was filling out.

He looked more like the playboy now than the recluse.

'Are you really that much of a coward, *Principessa*?' he murmured.

Adrenaline kicked and throbbed in my veins at the taunt.

But suddenly I realised something that made this man different from the playboy. I couldn't see the easy confidence he had used like a shield once upon a time. Instead, his face was grim, the charm stripped away to leave only intensity.

'Why would you leave now?' he growled, still taunting me, that dark gaze roaming over my features and down to the towel I had clutched to my breasts. 'When we both know the chemistry is still there.'

My nipples tightened, the adrenaline rush becoming hot and fluid and firing over my chilled skin.

The comment was insulting, his purpose clear. But there was something about the way he said it, the naked need I could see in his eyes, and the tension in his jaw that beckoned to the foolish girl. And made me believe that one thing had changed most of all... Now we were equals.

The need tightened like a vice in my abdomen. I should have stepped away from him, broken the live-wire connection, but I couldn't, the yearning in my chest sharp and brutal.

I shook my head, trying to shake away the drugging effects of his nearness and the desire which tugged at my insides.

'I... I can't,' I said.

I couldn't make this mistake again, this wasn't why I had come here...

Or was it?

The voice in my head goaded me, as I wrapped my arms tightly around my waist, trying to hold in all the wayward emotions which wanted to spill out. Emotions I thought I had conquered years ago.

'Then why did you come back to me?' he asked, his eyes still bright with desire and determination. But his voice was low with barely leashed anger. 'Did you pity me, *Principessa*? Did you come to gloat at my downfall?'

'*What*? No. Of course not,' I protested, shocked he would even think such a thing.

'Then why are you here? And why did you lie about who you were?'

I opened my mouth, to tell him about the pregnancy, the baby I had lost? The baby *we* had lost? But the words got trapped inside me. I didn't want his pity either.

It occurred to me, I didn't really know this tortured, taciturn man—any more than I had known the careless playboy. Even after five long weeks of cooking for him, of watching him work so hard to heal, I still didn't know who he was. But—god help me—I wanted to.

I couldn't find an answer for him. Because I wasn't even sure what the answer was myself anymore.

My bare feet sank into the sand, the feeling of vulnerability as scary as the potent heat scalding my insides.

The moonlight made his features look saturnine as he frowned.

'I don't know why,' I admitted at last, because I couldn't tell him the truth, couldn't even acknowledge it myself. Because it would be a betrayal of the woman I had worked so hard to become. The woman who would never have fallen for the slick charms of a man like him again. A man who could discard her so easily and leave her broken without a backwards glance.

Except was he still that man? What if *he* had changed too? What if there could be more between us now than there ever had been before?

He let out a rough laugh.

'You say you don't know, *Principessa*. As if the answer is not simple.' He captured my shoulder in one hard hand, making heat sweep to my core. Then glided his thumb under the edge of the towel, to touch my cleavage. Possessive, demanding, but with a sense of entitlement that was strangely beguiling.

His touch was electrifying, calling to all those foolish needs he had triggered so easily once before. But when he spoke, the words were rough and husky with the same need I felt.

'This is what we both need,' he said. 'Do you know I recognised you, the first time I saw you again—even though I refused to admit it—because I could still feel this need.'

The whispered confession seemed somehow important to my dazed mind, while the pheromones fired through my system triggered by his confident touch.

'I realise now, you are why I have worked so hard to become a man again. Instead of a pathetic excuse for one.' The resentment in his tone, the self-loathing shocked me, but not as much as the sense of stunned validation when he added, 'You are the only woman I have truly desired since that night, *Principessa*.'

Before I had a chance to question the logic of what he was saying, or my reaction to it, I let go of the towel. Offering myself to him. Wanting to finally feed this incessant hunger too.

The cove was warm, the night air sultry, but even so I shuddered as the protective layer dropped onto the sand. I couldn't deny the swell of euphoria in my chest. At the thought that I did matter to him even if I knew it was a layover from that little girl whose mother had abandoned her, and whose father had never wanted to know her. The little girl who had always yearned for affection—yearned to belong to someone.

'Why should I believe you?' I asked, forcing myself not to get swept up in those emotions again.

'Let me show you,' he said, then he wrapped his arm around my waist, to tug my body against the hard line of his—and I felt the press of his erection against my belly.

His mouth hovered close enough for me to see the purpose in his gaze as he whispered, 'If this is not what you want, you must tell me now.'

I lifted my chin and gave the only answer I could. 'I do want it.'

His lips slanted across mine and his tongue plundered.

I reached up, and sank my fingers into his hair, dragging him closer as my body ignited with the longing I had spent years denying. But refused to deny any longer.

Unlike before, his kiss wasn't practiced, or subtle, it was ruthless and demanding and more than a little desperate. His tongue drove into my mouth, exploring and exploiting every hidden recess, moving in a devastating rhythm.

I clung to his tall frame, my cool flesh warmed by the scorching heat of his.

We broke apart, both breathing heavily. He found the straps of my swimsuit, tugged them down. As he exposed the damp flesh to the warm night, all I could do was absorb the brutal ripples of sensation firing through my body.

Suddenly I was naked to the waist, my breasts swollen, the nipples achingly tight. He cupped the flesh, brushed his thumb over a nipple, then leant down to capture the tip in warm lips. I bucked in his arms, vicious sensation arrowing down, and threaded my fingers into the thick locks of hair.

He feasted for what felt like hours but could only have

been moments, as the yearning tension gripped my core, releasing the rush of liquid warmth.

I was shuddering and shaking when he finally lifted his head, no longer able to grasp where we were or what I was doing, only knowing that I wanted more—that I wanted it all, that I needed to feel him inside me again.

He stumbled slightly as he straightened and I clasped his arm. 'Are you okay?' I asked, concerned about his leg.

'Of course!'

I felt the slap of his rejection, but before I could react, he grabbed my wrist and pulled me towards one of the loungers on the beach.

'Take off your costume,' he said, fishing a small foil packet out of the pocket of his sweatpants.

I was shocked by the urgency of the husky demand, and the fact he had come prepared.

I clasped my arms over my naked breasts. Had he come here planning to seduce me? And what was going to happen once we had slaked this hunger?

But as he flung away his T-shirt, my mind blurred again, the urgent questions forgotten in the hot wave of arousal as the giddy desire battered me.

His chest was burnished by moonlight, the skin not as tanned as it had once been, the muscles leaner but no less magnificent. The old scars and tattoos I remembered were still there, but joined now by new marks, new wounds, from the crash. Compassion welled in my throat as I saw him wince, forced to put his weight on his injured leg to strip off his sweatpants.

But then I watched transfixed, as he rolled the condom on the heavy, thrusting erection.

The hot brick in my stomach sank deeper into my abdomen, throbbing and glowing as I lifted my face to his.

Did it matter if he had planned this? When I wanted it too? Perhaps this was what I had needed, all along. A chance to have him one more time, before I left this place forever.

He clasped my chin, lifted my face to stare into my eyes, his body vibrating now with the visceral tension I could feel gripping me too.

'Why are you not naked?' he asked, the fierce need in his eyes shocking me into action.

I stood to strip off the damp spandex. But a wave of shyness washed over me as he watched me. I held the costume to my chest, still unsure, still scared, by the force of my hunger.

He took the costume out of my hands and threw it away.

'Lie down,' he said.

I did as he asked, as it occurred to me he was struggling to move freely. Was his leg starting to hurt, after standing on it for so long? But as I opened my mouth to ask, he joined me on the lounger and pressed a finger to my lips.

'Do not be concerned, I promise I will not disappoint you.' There was an edge to his voice, both angry and defensive.

It wasn't my own pleasure I was concerned about, but I trapped the thought inside my mind. This was about sex, for both of us. It had to be. That was the only connection we had ever shared. I couldn't romanticise this moment. Couldn't allow myself to feel more for him than I should.

So when he lifted my hips, I wrapped my legs eagerly around his waist, opened myself for him, determined to make this all about pleasure too.

He grunted, probing with the thick head of his erection, then sank deep inside me in one powerful thrust.

I groaned, the fullness immense, the intimacy of our joining overwhelming as he pressed his face against my neck, his breathing harsh and shallow.

He swore in Italian, the words guttural and hoarse, then began to move. This time, unlike that night four years ago, the roll of his hips was clumsy, frantic, erratic, but no less forceful. I clung to him, the pleasure sparking and swelling as he pressed against a spot only he had ever found. I held on, the orgasm already shockingly close.

He pumped into me, once, twice and already I was cresting. I bowed up, cried out, the pleasure charging through me with startling intensity.

He shouted out his own release, then dropped on top of me, his heavy weight crushing me into the lounger, his body trembling, shaking, the still huge erection softening inside me.

I lay still, my body sore, the afterglow fading fast to be replaced with shock. How could the sexual connection between us still be so intense, so vivid, so immediate?

He rolled off me, then sat up, tugging his fingers through his hair, his head bent, his back rigid. He looked exhausted. But I stopped myself from reaching out to touch him, swallowed down the urge to ask him if he was okay.

I shouldn't care. I couldn't care. The fear gripped me again.

I scrambled off the lounger, desperate to return to the safety of my small villa, to finish my packing and leave first thing in the morning.

I scooped the towel up and wrapped it around myself. He hadn't said anything, the silence between us even more oppressive than the huge lump of anguish pressing against my chest.

I snatched up my swimsuit. This had been a mistake. A stupid, pathetic mistake. Thank goodness he couldn't run after me on his bad leg. But I walked too close to the lounger and he grabbed my arm.

'*Era buona per te?*' he asked, his voice raw.

'I'm sorry, I don't speak Italian,' I said, stupidly polite.

His thumb rubbed the hammering pulse in my wrist. 'I am asking you, Jessie,' he murmured, using my given name for the first time since I had known him. Why did that feel significant when it shouldn't? 'Did you climax?'

Heat fired into my cheeks. I was so surprised by the question, and the uncertainty in his tone, which was so unlike the man I had once known, who was always so confident about his ability to please a woman, I was speechless for a moment.

'I… Yes. I did,' I managed at last, the lump—now jammed in my throat—making it hard to get the words out.

He nodded, the relief on his face, and the flash of vulnerability, shocking me even more.

A rueful smile tugged at his lips. 'It has been a long time,' he said. '*Too* long. It seems I must work at this too. I will do better next time.'

Next time?

The stupid lump expanded and I knew I couldn't risk a next time. It had been a very long time for me too. Far too long. But I could never tell him he was the only man I had ever slept with. It would only leave me even more exposed and powerless.

'I'm tired. I should go to bed.' I struggled against his hold and he let me go. He was weary too.

'We will speak more of this tomorrow, yes?' he said. It sounded more like a demand than a request. Some things about him would never change, I realised.

'Sure,' I lied, stupidly grateful when he made no move to stop me as I dashed away.

I rushed up the steps carved into the rock wall. And I didn't look back. The soreness between my thighs was nothing compared to the choking sensation in my throat.

It was not until I got back to the housekeeper's cottage, and stood in the shower, that the raw sobs finally burst out of my mouth.

I sank down in the shower cubicle, let the hot water pound over me—washing away the scent of salt and him. I hugged my knees to my chest, tight, as my body was wracked by the wrenching sobs I had held in for too long.

For the pregnancy I had lost. But also for the girl I had once been. Who was so eager to be wanted, she had invested far more in that long ago encounter than she had ever realised until now.

Enough to want to bring that girl back, if only for one night.

But that girl was long gone, I realised, as I dragged my aching body out of the shower, climbed into bed and set my phone alarm, so I could leave the estate tomorrow before Renzo knew I was gone.

But when I finally tumbled into sleep, my dreams were haunted by dark, and devastatingly erotic visions. Of the Renzo from long ago, and the Renzo I knew now, who was as broken as I was. But who could still make me ache for more.

CHAPTER TEN

Jessie

WHEN I WOKE the next day, my body was sore and my heart still too tender from my shocking encounter with Renzo on the beach the night before—and the exhausting aftermath. It didn't take me long to realise I'd slept through my alarm.

I forced myself out of bed, to finish packing. Why hadn't I finished packing last night? Instead of indulging in a point-less crying jag?

After locking up the cottage, I slung my backpack over my shoulder and pulled my phone out, planning to call a cab to pick me up at the chateau gates, when a notification popped up, reminding me I was supposed to be briefing the new chef this morning before I left.

Panic made my palms sweat as I shoved the phone back into my pocket.

How could I have forgotten? It was close to seven o'clock, but the guy wasn't due to arrive until nine, because I had also planned to cook Renzo one last breakfast.

But I didn't want to see Renzo again, since I was way too shaky still about last night.

I had wanted closure. And that was what I'd achieved, I decided. Just in a much more graphic way than I had in-tended.

But I couldn't quite let go of my professional responsibility to do a good job—for the man I was about to run away from.

So I raced up to the house, ignoring all the places my body still ached. After dumping my backpack in the entrance hall, ready to make a quick getaway, I dashed to the kitchens, taking the long route through the house to avoid passing the doorway to the downstairs gym where Renzo would already be working with his physio.

My chest tightened as I walked into the cavernous kitchen which I had made my own in the past five weeks.

I stared stupidly at the pots of herbs I'd been growing on the windowsill, the shelves neatly stacked with the preserves, sauces and spice mixes I had made.

I wrote a quick note for the new chef, giving him my contact details so he could call me over the next few days while he settled in. Then I set about making a tray of home-made granola, fresh fruit and coffee which I could get one of the cleaning crew to take to Renzo's suite when he had finished his workout… By which time I planned to be miles away.

But just as I was quartering some fresh figs, a low voice from the doorway sent alarm skittering through my system.

'Buon giorno, Principessa.'

The loud clatter of the knife dropping onto the board was nowhere near as loud as the clattering of my own heartbeat.

Renzo was propped casually against the kitchen door frame. The black T-shirt and dark blue jeans, the clean-shaven jaw and the way his emerald eyes seemed to smile at me, as his gaze skated over me, made him look even more like the playboy I had once known. Which did not help one bit with my galloping pulse.

'Hi, I… I thought you'd be in the gym,' I said, my heart throbbing so hard now I could barely breathe.

Had we really made love last night in the cove?

Not made love, I corrected myself swiftly. Had wild, frantic sex.

I might have been able to convince myself I'd imagined the whole thing, if not for the residual hum of sensation triggered by his presence now. Or the tug of emotion which became a vicious yank when he pushed away from the door frame and limped into the room.

'I had more important business here,' he said as he sat on one of the stools on the corner of the large kitchen island. He was so close now I could smell the tangy citrus scent of his shampoo, see the flicker of knowledge and arousal in his gaze.

'Surely there's nothing more important than your physiotherapy,' I mumbled, grabbing the knife again, determined to ignore the huge lump forming in my throat.

If only I could have avoided seeing him again. But nothing could ever be easy where Renzo was concerned, apparently.

He leant over, took the knife from my grasp and placed it back on the board. Then he picked up my hand in warm, callused fingers and gave it a gentle tug, forcing my gaze to his.

'Do you know why I do the therapy?' he asked me.

I frowned, the non sequitur confusing me.

'To get better,' I said. Was this a trick question? Why hadn't I just run when I had the chance?

He stroked his thumb over the back of my hand. The contact was both gentle and yet electrifying, and I couldn't control the shiver of reaction.

A smile twitched on his lips. And I knew he had felt it too.

'I do the therapy so I can become who I was. Or as close as I can get to who I was before the crash.'

I nodded. 'Okay,' I said. Not sure why he was telling me this.

'But there is something else I lost. My appetite—which is something only you can help me get back.'

I tugged my hand free, feeling trapped and wary and needy... But worst of all was the trickle of disappointment—which was silly—at the memory of him telling me the night before he had worked on the therapy to become the man he had been, for me.

I had been *hired* to cook for him. Nothing more. He'd probably only said that last night because he had wanted to sleep with me, and to be fair it had totally worked.

'I'm not the only person who can cook for you,' I said, making it clear I didn't care that was all he had ever really wanted of me. 'You'll like the guy who's replacing me.' I said, struggling to remain professional, and unmoved. 'He's Italian. He was the head chef in a restaurant in Rome called Deliziosa, one of the best in the region. You're going to adore his tiramisu, it's...'

He pressed a finger to my lips, cutting off the unconvincing babble.

'That is not the appetite I am talking of, *Principessa*.'

I blinked, my cheeks flushing at the blatant hunger in his gaze.

'I... That's... Last night was a mistake.' My embarrassment was made worse by the deep pulsing at my core—and the memory of my startlingly swift orgasm, almost as soon as he had entered me. 'Last night. That's not what I was hired for,' I managed, all but choking on my mortification now.

To my horror, his smile spread into a grin and he started to chuckle. His husky laughter was so much more relaxed and natural than when he had first laughed in my presence all those weeks ago. But I refused to be beguiled by it.

'This is good, is it not?' he said, finally controlling his

amusement. 'Or that would make me a man who pays women for sex.' He laughed some more at my expense. 'I have done many things I am not proud of, *Principessa*. But this is not one of them.'

His mocking tone, and the sparkle of humour in his eyes, had my temper fraying. After a virtually sleepless night, and my frantic desperation to get out of here as quickly as possible, I was so not in the mood to be the butt of his jokes.

I untied my apron. 'I need to leave. You can make your own breakfast. I'm not being paid for today anyway,' I announced, slapping the apron onto the countertop.

But as I tried to march past him, he caught my wrist.

'I apologise, *Principessa*,' he said, tugging me forward, until I found myself trapped between his strong thighs. I could still see the twinkle of amusement in his eyes, but it was the hooded emotion in his gaze which disturbed me more. 'Do not be upset.'

I struggled against his hold, aware of his scent, his nearness, the ripple of arousal becoming a wave.

'You just called me a prostitute,' I said, hating the defensiveness in my voice, the obvious overreaction to his words which I couldn't seem to control, because my emotions were still in turmoil from last night. Unlike his. 'I think I've got a right to be upset.'

His smile died, and for a moment a stricken look flashed across his face, but it was gone so fast I was sure I had imagined it.

'On the contrary,' he said carefully, the smile returning, but looking less amused now. 'I said this is what you are not. I do not forget I was your first lover, *Principessa*.'

I sighed and stopped fighting against his hold.

Not that again.

Surely, he couldn't feel responsible for taking my virginity.

'That was a long time ago,' I said. 'I'm certainly not a virgin anymore,' I added, trying to sound as assertive—and jaded—as I could.

The last thing I wanted him to know was that he was still the only man I'd ever slept with. Because then he would want to know why. And I didn't want to tell him about the miscarriage. The pregnancy I had lost which had only ever been real to me. Because somehow that pain felt too intimate, and too personal.

Not only that, but if he knew he was still my only lover, it would probably turbocharge his ego. And it looked as if that was more than robust enough again after last night.

He cupped my chin, tilted my face up so I was forced to meet his gaze.

'So, if you are no longer new to sex,' he said carefully. 'You will know, last night was not good.' The smile on his lips contradicted the intensity in his gaze. 'Or not as good as it should have been. I should have taken my time. You are a woman I wish to feast on, and instead I devoured you in a few quick bites. Much as I did with your delicious food when I first tasted it.'

Is he actually serious right now?

Heat flared across my collarbone, which was not really selling my "I'm totally a woman of the world" shtick. But it was the best I could do in the circumstances. I'd never had such an intimate conversation before with anyone. One that was freaking me out and turning me on at the same time.

'I had an orgasm, Renzo,' I managed, surprised I didn't spontaneously combust at the thought of how quickly I had come—which was surely just one more indication of how susceptible I still was to his touch, even if he was out of practice. 'I'm not complaining. Really, you have nothing more to prove.' I glanced down at his crotch, struggling to appear as confident as he was. 'Everything's in good working order again,' I added, my throat drying to parchment, as I spotted the solid bulge in his lap stretching the worn denim.

My gaze snapped back to his face. Was Renzo getting turned on too?

'So, you can consider yourself good to go,' I finished, trying to sound flippant, although something twisted inside me at the thought of all the other women who would probably share his bed again now he had rediscovered his libido.

He wasn't mine, and he never had been. Nor did he want to be. This conversation wasn't about intimacy, not really, it was about sex—and how he wanted to use me to practice his moves again. If anything, I should be insulted not aroused.

Which just made it all the more annoying I could still feel that stupid bubble of anticipation and desire expanding inside me.

A quick grin appeared on his lips, and the intensity in his eyes softened, but he didn't release his grip on my wrist.

'Working order? Yes. And for that I am glad. But good? No, I don't think so. There is much more I have to prove. And I wish to prove it with you.'

'Wha-what?' My face flared so hot I was pretty sure it could probably be seen from space now. Worse than my mortification, though, was the deep needy pulsing in my core at the implication he thought I was somehow special, or different. When I knew I wasn't.

I yanked my arm out of his grasp, and stepped away from him.

'No,' I said, as demonstrably as I could manage when my insides seemed to be melting into hot lava. Hot aching, yearning lava. 'Really, I'm glad I could help you out with your...' I flicked my gaze over his physique again, then stopped abruptly.

Don't look at the bulge, you idiot.

I locked my gaze firmly onto his face.

'Your performance issues,' I managed, feeling increasingly aroused and increasingly ridiculous. Never a great combination. 'But now I really have to get going.'

He snagged my wrist, again, before I could make my getaway.

'Don't go, Jessie, I need you here, still. For more than just sex.'

His voice had the same edge it had had last night. The edge that told me how hard it was for him to admit a vulnerability.

Ignore it. He's fine.

But I couldn't quite bring myself to yank my wrist free again, my ribs tightening around my heart like a vice.

'Honestly, Renzo. You'll like Matteo's cooking, you will, he's really good,' I said, because surely that could be the only other reason he still needed me to stay. He liked my cooking *a lot.* I knew that.

'It is not your cuisine I am talking of.' He shook his head, the gruff laugh self-deprecating, and all the more beguiling as a result. 'Henri insists I must show my face in public again.' His jaw tensed, and I could see irritation, but also the brief flash of—if not panic, certainly discomfort. 'The company's stock has been dropping, ever since the crash. Rumours have been whispered that I am not who I was. That I have lost the drive that made me a good investment. So, I must stop hiding.' He sounded annoyed, but then his expression became strangely unreadable. 'Dante Allegri and his wife are holding an exclusive event at his casino in Monte

Carlo, in three weeks' time. A ball. There will be investors there. Celebrities. VIPs. Henri has begged me to attend to destroy these rumours. If I go, I will need a date. But I have no wish to see the pity in the eyes of women I have dated before. You are the only one I wish to have on my arm.'

I was so surprised at the request, I didn't know what to say for a moment. The thought of being invited to such a prestigious event was exciting, but the thought of being asked by Renzo even more so. A stupid bubble of hope joined the boulder of emotion in my throat, at the thought he might need me. *Really* need me. Not just for my cooking skills, or to practice his skills in bed, but as a companion, a friend, a lover?

'You... You're asking me on a date? To the Allegri Ball,' I said, dumbly, just to clarify I hadn't got it totally wrong. 'But I work for you,' I added when he nodded. 'Won't that just start more rumours?'

'Belle and Galanti will be there, and you are her cousin. We can use this to explain how we met.' He frowned, searching my face and I suddenly had the terrible thought he could see right through me, to the needy girl beneath—who had always wanted to be noticed, to be seen, to be important. Not just to her mother, and her father, but also to him.

How had he found the perfect way to make me feel needed? I dismissed the terrifying thought, that he could read me so easily.

Why would he bother? He was asking me for practical help, with his business. This request wasn't really personal, despite what had happened last night.

Weirdly, the thought he needed my help for purely pragmatic reasons made it feel safer to be tempted, to want so much to say yes.

'And you are not my employee anymore,' he continued;

drawing his thumb across my bottom lip. I sighed, before I could stop myself. 'Your contract ended yesterday, is that not so?' he added, the fierce, but effortlessly charming grin making my pulse accelerate, and sink into my panties. 'And I do not pay you for sex. This we have already agreed,' he continued, sealing our deal with a clever logic. 'If you stay until the ball we can have three weeks to enjoy ourselves. We have both earned it, no? Three weeks more is all I ask of you, then we will go our separate ways.'

He captured my hips and tugged me back into the space between his thighs, making me far too aware of his big body, the hard contours of his chest which had become more defined in the past month, as he'd worked so hard to make himself whole again. The tantalising scent which had always tormented me filled my lungs as I gathered a staggered breath, trying to think past the adrenaline rush of being wanted, being needed, being asked to stay. Here, with him. Not as his chef, but as his…?

I frowned. What exactly would I be? But then the realisation of what he was really asking slammed into me. I would be his *lover*.

I drew in another ragged breath. And held the thought in my head.

I would be Renzo Camaro's lover for three whole weeks. I could get to know him better, and get the opportunity to ask all those nagging questions about him which I'd had not just over the last five weeks, but also over the years since we had spent that one incredible night together. I could finally get answers for all the things that young woman had wanted to know when she had woken up in his luxury bedroom and found him gone.

I had been through so much after that one night—as a result of the pregnancy and the miscarriage—which had made our night together much more significant than it should have been. But I could see now, I'd been holding all those questions inside me ever since. Perhaps I deserved to have them answered now? Once and for all?

That said, the thought of being Renzo's lover for real was as terrifying as it was exhilarating.

I didn't want to get hung up on him or risk opening up old wounds.

But had those old wounds ever really been about Renzo? I wondered. And if our liaison had a definite end date, three weeks from now, surely I wouldn't have time to get *too* invested in this relationship?

Like every one of Renzo's other relationships, what he was offering me wasn't going to be permanent. That was not what he wanted, and it was not what I needed either.

So why couldn't I do this? If I already knew the risks? And was prepared for them? Why shouldn't I take this chance? To finally get the closure I'd been looking for all along?

He cradled my cheek, stroked the skin, sending sensation shimmering and shivering through my body.

'Will you stay, *Principessa*? With me? For three weeks? And then we will part after the ball? *Per favore*,' he added, his tone raw.

Per favore. Please. The few words in Italian I could translate.

I felt a strange sense of release, as a smile tugged at my lips and seeped into my heart.

Why had I never seen it before? We really were equals now, more than we had ever been before. Because the truth was, we both needed closure from that night. He had suffered a great deal in the years since that night too, just as I had. We were both broken in our own way. What harm could it do, to try and fix ourselves together? Before we parted? To indulge the chemistry we shared? So I could finally move on, for real, and start to contemplate dating another man, a man who would be able to cherish me the way Renzo could not? If I could do that, maybe I could even have the family I had always yearned for too, children, a life partner like Alexi was to Belle... My life had been stalled since that night, because I had developed a strange obsession with Renzo as a result of an accidental pregnancy that hadn't even lasted. Surely I had to take this chance to finally move on with my life, for good.

I nodded.

'*Si?*' He grinned.

'Yes, okay, I'll stay. For three weeks. And be your date for the ball.'

'*Bene,*' he murmured, his eyes sparkling with a delight that made the boulder expand in my throat. I blinked furiously. And ignored it.

For goodness' sake, don't you dare cry. That's not what this is about.

He clasped the back of my neck, and kissed me, with a fervour that took my breath away. When we finally broke apart, we were both breathless.

'I will have the staff put your luggage in my suite today,' he announced.

I swallowed the blip of panic. 'Perhaps I should stay in the housekeeper's cottage,' I offered, unsure again, knowing I wasn't comfortable moving into his room.

'Why?' he asked, genuinely perplexed.

'It's... It just feels weird, me living in the house, in your bedroom, I guess.' I struggled to explain without sounding silly. Or worse, coy.

The puzzled expression became rueful, and amused. 'Jessie, I want to have you in my bed.' He lifted my palm to his lips and bit into the soft flesh beneath my thumb.

Sensation streaked through me and I gasped. His answering smile was more than a little self-satisfied. 'This is what you want too, *si*?'

'Well, yes,' I was forced to admit, even though I now felt impossibly gauche and transparent—and out of my depth. Again.

'The housekeeper's villa is too far away,' he explained carefully. 'And anyway, you will not be my chef anymore, but my guest.'

I nodded, closing my fingers into a fist, in an attempt to contain the sensation.

It felt wonderful but also frightening to be the centre of Renzo's attention. Why hadn't I factored that in when I had agreed to become his lover? Probably because I'd never been any man's lover before now. It was a whole new experience—that was all. An experience I had no idea how to negotiate.

'Actually, perhaps I should keep working then. While I'm here,' I offered, trying to find a way to manage my panic without looking even more clueless.

His brows shot up his forehead, then flattened in a frown. 'This is foolish, no? I do not wish for you to work, but to be available. So that we can enjoy ourselves.'

Available?

It was obvious he was not at all happy with my suggestion. But while I was totally on board with us enjoying the chemistry between us for the next three weeks—because that throbbing in my sex was not going away anytime soon—the thought of just sitting around all day while he did his physio, then being ready to put out whenever he wanted felt…well, wrong. We wouldn't be equals anymore. I would be at his beck and call. And I didn't like that thought. At all.

But more than that…

I didn't want to have too much time to ponder our relationship… Not relationship, I corrected myself quickly. Our *affair*.

Also, I was not an idle person. I'd always worked, ever since I was thirteen and I had got my first job at the local chip shop, peeling and chopping potatoes before school, so I could get free food, and help with the bills my mum often forgot to pay. Plus, it was already going to feel super weird when the rest of the staff realised what was going on—without me swanning about the house with nothing to do all day.

It would still be super awkward, of course, if I carried on working in the kitchen while also sleeping with the boss, and I was sure there would be more than a few raised eyebrows. But I wouldn't feel so compromised. Because at least I would still have a role here, other than being his mistress.

His mistress.

I pushed the word away. But even so, it made me remember my mum, and the awful guys she had attached herself to, because she had craved male affection and wanted someone to look after her, because she was scared of being alone, of surviving on her own. I had always refused to be like her—which had to be why the thought of being Renzo's 'guest' felt so wrong.

'I can't move into your bedroom, Renzo.' I said. 'And I'd really like to carry on working for you. If that's okay.'

'This is madness.' He huffed, and I could see he was exasperated, but I knew I couldn't back down. 'And not convenient.'

He clasped my hips and pulled me closer to nuzzle the pulse point in my neck and make me ache.

'I adore the food you cook for me…' he added, the husky tenor of his voice doing devastating things to my insides. 'But I like the taste of you more.'

I placed my hands against his broad chest, felt the distracting ripple of muscle as I pushed him back.

'Please, Renzo. It's important to me,' I said, my voice firm, or as firm as it could be while his hands were wandering up my waist, his magic thumbs gliding under my T-shirt.

He frowned again, but then the smile returned, and I could see calculation as well as determination. 'What about the chef who has been hired to replace you?' he asked, all innocence.

Oh, damn. It was my turn to frown. How could I have forgotten about Matteo Galvini? Who was due to arrive in an hour expecting to take over my kitchen.

'Maybe you're right, maybe I should just go?' I said, stupidly devastated at the thought of leaving, but somehow knowing I couldn't agree to this *affair* on his terms.

I stepped back, but he grasped my hips to drag me back towards him.

'No, you cannot leave, we will find a compromise,' he announced. The smile was gone, replaced with grim determination. And some silly corner of my heart was flattered, that this arrangement seemed to mean enough for him to bend, when I knew he was not a man who liked to bend. *Ever.*

'What if you cook in the morning and he cooks in the evening?' he said. 'Then we can have the nights at least.' I could see he wasn't happy with the compromise. But my heart leapt at the thought he was trying to find a solution. For me.

'That could work,' I said, excitement firing through my veins. 'That could totally work. If Mr Galvini is okay with that arrangement.'

'I will speak to Henri and have him change the contract,' he said. 'Do not worry, Galvini will be very pleased with this arrangement.'

I wasn't exactly sure what that meant, but I didn't question him. I didn't want to leave. And I was impossibly flattered he was willing to make this work. For both of us.

'But I want you closer than the housekeeper's villa,' he added, wrapping his arms around my waist. And kissing me lightly. 'This is not negotiable, Jessie,' he continued, and it was clear from the look in his eyes, he was not going to bend much more than he already had.

I nodded. 'Okay, how about if I move into a suite near yours? Would that work?' I offered, happy to negotiate too now, knowing I had already got a rare concession out of him.

Doesn't make you special, Jess, just remember that.

He stared at me for the longest time. But then he sighed. 'You drive a very hard bargain, *Principessa*,' he said, still sounding exasperated.

The feeling of validation. Of approval. That I had managed to bargain with him. That I hadn't just capitulated, made my chest feel tight.

'I know,' I said, not quite able to contain my grin of triumph. 'Have we got a deal?' I asked, echoing his earlier question. *'Per favore,'* I added, cheekily.

He huffed out a laugh. 'I have created a monster, I think.'

'Yup.' I just smiled back, more than a little smug.

He gave another long-suffering sigh. *'Bene*, I will tell the staff to move your luggage into the suite *next* to mine.'

'Great,' I said, the adrenaline rush immense. But before I had a chance to celebrate my victory, he yanked me into his arms and sealed our deal with a kiss so raw and urgent, I was a mass of pulsating sensations—and vivid and confusing emotions—when he finally released me.

'Do not be surprised if I visit you there, *often*,' he said, the dark need in his eyes making the adrenaline rush turbocharged.

'Okay,' I said.

He was reaching for me again, when his phone buzzed. He swore and let me go.

After reading the notification, he shoved the mobile back into his pocket. 'I must go to the gym.' He nodded towards the breakfast tray I had been preparing for him. 'Have someone send that down to the gym. Not you...' he added pointedly, then glanced down at his crotch. 'The work is already difficult enough.'

A blush bloomed again in my cheeks as I noticed the prominent ridge in his jeans.

Oh...my.

'Do not look so smug. I will get my revenge tonight.' He laughed—the sound rueful and yet full of wicked promise—as he placed me away from him, and headed towards the door, his limp more pronounced than usual.

'Addio, Principessa.' He threw the words over his shoulder, sounding more relaxed and happy than he had since I had first arrived at the chateau.

My heart thundered in my chest, and floated into my throat, as I set about finishing off the breakfast tray before the new chef arrived.

I didn't feel smug, I realised, I felt light too. Lighter than I had in years—as the next three weeks stretched out before me, full of possibilities and promise. And the chance to finally let go of the sadness which had haunted me for far too long.

CHAPTER ELEVEN

Renzo

'RENZO, THIS IS WONDERFUL, I'm so glad you are finally going to socialise again. I'll have Carmine inform the Allegris you are attending the ball and get him to make all the necessary arrangements.'

The enthusiasm and excitement in Henri's voice made me wince—the last thing I wanted to do was attend a ball when I could no longer dance. And I'd had no intention of accepting the invitation until this morning. But when I had seen the stubborn refusal in Jessie's eyes I had been forced to come up with a way to persuade her to stay, and the idea of inviting her to the Allegri event had popped into my head before I could think of a better one.

But once I had suggested it, it had seemed like a perfect strategy. Because I had discovered something vitally important about my beautiful chef in the last few weeks. Jessie Burton was a people pleaser. A fixer. A person who wanted to help. Someone who, behind that fiercely independent exterior, was kind and loyal and—I swallowed around the tightness in my throat—sweet. Not the sort of woman I would ever have been drawn to, once upon a time, but for whatever reason it appeared she was the only woman I wanted right now.

I knew I was using her tender nature, her soft-heartedness against her to get what I wanted, and if I had not wanted her so much, I might have felt badly about that. But when she had agreed to stay, I hadn't regretted my actions... Until now. As the thought of what attending the ball would actually entail began to sink in.

But I would have three weeks with her, before I had to face that ordeal. And who knows how things would be between us by then? In truth, the Allegri Ball would not be so much of an ordeal, with her by my side. And it was an ordeal I would have to face anyway sooner or later. I had not lied to her about the need to be seen in public again. I needed to step back into the spotlight, if not only to save my company, but also certainly to start rebuilding my life as it had been before the crash.

The reason my former life seemed shallow and unappealing to me now was surely only because I had been away from it for so long. Once I returned to the social whirl, it would feel as if I had never left. And hopefully I would begin to enjoy it again.

'Tell Carmine to let the Allegris know I will be attending the event with a date,' I announced.

'C'est merveilleux.' I could hear Henri's surprise on the other end of the phone. 'Can I give Carmine a name?'

'Jessie Burton,' I said, ignoring the tinge of guilt.

'The chef?' The surprise had turned to shock.

'Si.'

Henri was silent for a long time. But if he disapproved of me dating an employee—something I had never done before—there was no sign of it in his voice when he replied.

'This is unexpected, Renzo. But good news. So I guess you *really* enjoyed her cooking then?' he added with a knowing laugh.

'*Oui,*' I said, without any humour. I did not find his insinuation funny.

Before the crash, Henri had often teased me about my shameless dating habits, but joking about Jessie made me feel uncomfortable.

My playboy reputation had been a source of pride for me once too—but it was less so now. The refreshing candour with which Jessie had bargained with me this morning—to preserve her pride and independence—suddenly made me ashamed of that man. She expected so little from me, it made me oddly determined to defy her expectations.

I frowned. Maybe that unfamiliar impulse would pass too, after three weeks of indulging ourselves.

'Tell Carmine he'll need to arrange a stylist,' I said, inspired as I recalled the small luggage I had noticed in the hall on my way to the gym this morning, which had had me immediately detouring to the kitchens.

The panic which had assailed me, at the thought she might be planning to run out on me, had only intensified when I had caught her there and spotted the note she had jotted down for the new chef. How I had managed to remain calm and persuasive I would never know, because my insides had been churning with a vicious combination of anger and fear. And desire.

Somehow, I had become fixated on her. On the brief night we had shared four years ago and on the time we had shared together since she had come back. Not to mention our frantic love-making in the cove. Enough to know I needed her—and only her—to help me return to myself the rest of the way.

There was something about the artless way she looked at me, that intoxicating mix of wariness and desire, which had already helped to rebuild my confidence, as a lover as well as a man. She had held nothing back last night, responding instantly to my touch, even though the whole encounter had been clumsy and rushed.

Is that why she had kept her identity a secret from me? Because she was scared of the intensity of our connection? I liked to think so. I also knew our chemistry was something I was going to take great pleasure in exploring properly over the next three weeks.

She was a beautiful, incredibly stimulating woman. But why would she not embrace that?

'I do not think she has the wardrobe to attend an event like the Allegris',' I said to Henri. I had only seen her in jeans and T-shirts and her luggage was not the kind to contain designer gowns. 'I want her to look stunning at the ball.' Because she *was* stunning, I thought, as I recalled the red dress which had once captivated me too.

No doubt it would be a major struggle to get her to accept my gift. She was nothing if not fiercely independent. But I would enjoy persuading her. Plus I was consumed by the desire to ensure she enjoyed the ball. It would be her reward, I decided, for being what I needed, when I needed it.

'No problem,' Henri replied. 'I will tell Carmine to hire a stylist. Do you have one in mind?'

'Just tell him to hire the best,' I said. 'Also, I'll be attending the next management meeting via a video link.'

'That's… Yes, Renzo! That would be incredible.' As I heard the pleasure in Henri's voice—who'd been begging me for months to get more involved in my businesses again— it occurred to me that my appetite for so many things had returned since Jessie Burton had come back into my life.

I dismissed the sentimental thought. I was not a romantic. But who knew sexual desire could be linked to so many other things? I did not, until I had lost it.

As I ended the call, I imagined what I would do to Jessie tonight, to make up for my poor performance yesterday. Tonight, I intended to feast on her as she deserved. I would make her beg for mercy. Then I would be another step closer to being the man I once was again.

A man in control of his own destiny.

Jessie

My fingers shook as I unpacked my small number of belongings and placed them in the heavy antique dresser in the suite which had been provided for me in the chateau. The sun had dipped towards the horizon, casting the redolent glow of twilight over the room's luxury furniture. Night was approaching and I hadn't seen Renzo all day, not since I had agreed to become his part-time mistress.

But the lightness I had felt then had disappeared during a long day of agonising over my decision.

What was I thinking? Believing this was a good—or even workable—arrangement?

I paused, as I placed the last of my underwear into the dresser.

Perhaps I should just tell him I'd changed my mind?

The truth was I'd become more and more aware how untenable the situation was, and how uncomfortable it made me feel, all day.

Even though the head of the cleaning crew, a young man called Eduardo, had been totally unfazed when he had informed me the suite had been made ready for me on Renzo's instructions, I had been mortified.

And then there was the moment when I had to tell Matteo, the new chef, that the terms of his employment had been changed and I would still be working during the day—so he would only be required to make the evening meal. Matteo was a nice man, and as we had worked on a list of menus together, he hadn't questioned the change in arrangements.

But still I felt guilty. And embarrassed.

So embarrassed, I couldn't bring myself to tell Matteo that Renzo and I were an item and he would be cooking supper for both of us tonight. So, I had snuck out of the house, and made myself scarce for the last three hours, going for a long walk in the grounds, then having a swim in one of the *other* coves, so I would not be in the chateau when Matteo served Renzo dinner.

When I had crept back into the house ten minutes ago, I had come up the back stairs to my new suite, careful not to pass the doorway to Renzo's rooms next door.

But all my doubts were coalescing in my stomach now like a ball of lead.

Was Renzo in his room? Waiting for me? Was he expecting me to turn up in a negligee or something? Ready for sex?

I huffed out a breath. For goodness' sake, I had no clue what my role here even was anymore. What was he expecting of me? What was I expecting from myself?

I had unpacked to get a handle of my nerves, but as I closed the dresser drawer, I pressed unsteady hands to my blazing cheeks.

This was ridiculous. I was so not cut out to be any man's mistress. Not even a part-time temporary one. Obviously, I couldn't do this.

You need to leave. Like, now! Duh.

I yanked the drawer back open, and grabbed the stack of underwear, but as I scooped it back out of the dresser, intending to run for the hills, a low voice had me spinning around.

'I missed you at supper, *Principessa*.'

I was so startled at the sight of Renzo leaning against the doorway to the room's terrace—the dying glow of sunset shining off his dark hair and making the tanned planes and angles of his face gleam—I sprayed the underwear across the bed.

'How…how did you get there?' I asked.

And how could he look so relaxed and so—I swallowed heavily, taking in the way the worn jeans and linen shirt only accentuated his muscular physique—and so impossibly gorgeous, when I was a complete wreck?

He hadn't even touched me yet and I could already feel the lava pooling in my abdomen.

'You nearly gave me a heart attack,' I added.

'Our suites have a shared terrazzo.' He sent me an assured smile, then stepped into the room as if he owned it—probably because he did. 'It will give us better access.'

Better access to what, exactly? I wanted to scream, but all my nerves were now wrapped around my throat, choking me.

He walked around the four-poster bed, the hitch in his stride only making the emotion knot tighter around my ribs. And the lava flow down between my thighs. As he reached me, he took the only item of clothing I still held out of my numbed fingers—a particularly fetching pair of bargain-basement blue cotton panties which the supermodels he used to date would never have been seen dead in—and lifted them to his nose.

He took a deep breath, and sighed. 'Mmm… They smell *deliziosa*,' he murmured in that gruff Italian accent which seemed to stroke my core, his gaze riveted to my burning face.

'They smell of laundry detergent you mean,' I blurted out, managing to release the stranglehold on my throat.

'No, *Principessa*.' Those tantalising lips quirked in an impossibly sensual smile, as he rubbed the clean cotton over my hot cheek. 'They smell of you.'

I stepped back, the emotion in my chest painful. Desire and approval were not the same thing. Why did I keep mixing them up?

This was all a hangover from my childhood, I decided. The father who had never wanted to know me. The mother who had eventually abandoned me too. Intellectually, I knew that, but even so I couldn't seem to clamp down on the brutal need enveloping my body and echoing in my heart when he looked at me this way. As if I really mattered to him.

I took the panties from him, wrapped them around my fingers, staring at them because I didn't want to look into his eyes and see the glow of desire, the purpose and determination to have me, to hold me, to make love to me.

'I've decided I think I should leave—this isn't going to work,' I said, my voice trembling with the embarrassment and confusion which had unsettled me all day.

He tucked a knuckle under my chin, lifted my gaze to his. 'I thought we had a deal, Jessie?'

There was no demand in his tone for once, just a sort of probing curiosity. But even so, the panic clawed at my throat.

'I know… But… I just can't…be here, like this… It's just not me… Not who I am. Not who I want to be.' I paused. I was babbling now, and not making a lot of sense. But I was scared he would persuade me to stay with the force of our chemistry, which was even now bombarding my senses. And making me want to fall into his arms, when I knew I should be running in the opposite direction.

But to my surprise, instead of taking advantage of the desire I couldn't seem to control, he sat on the bed. He straightened his injured leg, rubbed his thigh. Then he patted the space next to him. 'Sit. Tell me, what is the problem? And we will fix it.'

'Really?'

'Yes, of course.' His lips quirked. 'The next three weeks must be pleasurable for both of us. Or it will not work.'

He said it so simply, I felt foolish. And pathetic. He was right. It was only three weeks for goodness' sake. And this was about pleasure. Nothing more or less. Why had I spent the whole day freaking out?

And where exactly had the woman gone who had convinced herself she was totally Renzo's equal this morning? Why was I behaving like a blushing inarticulate virgin all of a sudden, instead of a woman with a career—who had been supporting herself since she was sixteen years old? Even longer if I considered how useless my mum had been, at doing anything other than bringing home the latest creep to 'look after us'—most of whom hadn't even been able to look after themselves.

Where had the Jessie gone who had survived a miscarriage?

I forced the wayward thought back into the box marked Ancient History before it could derail me too.

The miscarriage wasn't relevant now. Renzo had been the father of my baby, yes, but that's all he'd been. I had wanted him to know about the pregnancy at the time, because I had never really been sure if my own father had ever known about my existence—and that had added to my confusion and insecurity as a kid. But I hadn't needed or wanted Renzo's help or support. I had never been intending to rely on him. I was the one who had wanted that baby. And so it had seemed right that I had been the only one to mourn its loss.

I sat down next to him and fidgeted some more with the panties. Not sure what to say.

'What did you mean, that this is not who you are?' he asked, far too perceptively. 'Who are you tonight that you weren't this morning?'

I sighed, then forced myself to meet his gaze. I tried not to fall into that endless green before I could get out the words which have made me sick with embarrassment all day. 'I'm your mistress.'

His lips quirked, making him look both amused, but also puzzled. 'This is a very old-fashioned word to use,' he said. 'But does it not just mean you are my lover? Why do you find this insulting?'

'Because… You know.' I shrugged, the embarrassment starting to strangle me again. Did he really need me to spell it out?

'No, I do not. What does this word mean exactly in English?' he asked, sounding genuinely confused.

'That I'm your kept woman, that I'm here at your convenience. It makes me feel a bit powerless and pathetic if I'm honest. That I'm not *me* anymore.' I could imagine how naive and unsophisticated I probably sounded to him. Why couldn't I just chill out and enjoy the experience for three weeks? Was it because he was so rich? Or the fact I was also working for him? Or was my struggle more deep-rooted—did it go back to the virginal girl he had rejected so easily four years ago?

'But this is not true. You would not let me keep you here without insisting on working for me too,' he pointed out, still confused.

'Well, yes but…' Okay, he had a point. Sort of. But I could still feel the crippling embarrassment when I had left Matteo in the kitchen preparing dinner. 'I just… I missed dinner this evening because I couldn't bring myself to tell Matteo he was making dinner for both of us. After doing a professional job with him all afternoon, working on menus and talking him through everything in the kitchen, it just felt wrong to expect him to make dinner for me... With you.'

Surely, he had to see how weird that would be? How wrong?

But his lips twitched with amusement again. And then he placed his palm on my knee and rubbed, sending unwanted sensation shimmering to my core. Because of course it did.

'There is no need for you to tell Galvini of our arrangement,' he said, easily. 'As I have already done so.'

'You... Wh-what?' My mouth dropped open as heat scalded my cheeks. 'What did you say to him?' I asked, so horrified I could barely form the words.

He shrugged. 'That we are lovers and that I will expect him to cook a meal for both of us tomorrow evening.'

'You didn't!' The lead weight in my stomach rammed my throat as panic assailed me. How on earth was I going to face the other chef tomorrow afternoon, and appear professional and competent, when we were supposed to be going to the produce market in Villefranche-sur-Mer together?

'Oh god.' I sank my burning face into my hands. 'I can't believe you did that.'

This was just...*awful*. Awkward didn't even begin to cover it.

'Shh, you are overreacting, *Principessa*.' Renzo's arm wrapped around my shoulders and I heard his husky laugh. Which should have made me angry. But I was actually too horrified to feel anything but mortification at the moment. 'Galvini was not embarrassed, or upset by this news, so why are you?'

Well, of course, he hadn't *acted* like he was embarrassed

or upset, I wanted to scream. Renzo was a powerful man and he was also paying Matteo's wages.

'What exactly *did* he say?' I groaned, even though I was pretty sure I didn't want to know.

I heard the gruff laugh again. 'If you must know, he complimented me on my good fortune.'

'He what?' My gaze jerked to his, the rich glow of amusement and pride in his eyes making my already erratic heartbeat become loud and discordant. And the melting sensation between my thighs heat. 'He didn't?' I said, not sure I believed him. Was he trying to make me feel better now? Less awkward and exposed? Because if he was, it was working but I wasn't sure that was a good thing.

'Jessie,' he murmured, the affection in his tone doing something equally disturbing to my insides. He brushed his palm over my burning cheek, hooked an unruly tendril of hair behind my ear. 'Galvini is Italian. And a talented chef.' He grinned. 'Although not as talented as you of course,' he continued, the gentle tone doing nothing to ease the turmoil in my insides. 'He is a man of good taste, in all things,' he added, his gaze intensifying. 'Of course, this would be his response. But if he did dare to judge you, or me, I would have fired him on the spot.'

'That's my point exactly!' I said, horrified but also stupidly comforted by the fierce protectiveness in his expression. 'He couldn't say anything else.'

'Except this is not the point,' he disagreed, the smile disappearing. 'Galvini's reaction is not important. The point is, why is it important to you? He does not judge you, so why do you judge yourself? Is it that you are ashamed to be my lover?'

Hurt flickered in his eyes, throwing me back four years

to that awkward moment when we had first slept together, and I had insulted him without meaning to.

'No, not at all,' I said, glad when I saw the tension leave his face. 'It's not about you... I guess it's to do with my mother.'

'Tua madre?' His eyebrows rose. 'You think she would not approve?' he asked, clearly confused again as he searched my face looking for a coherent answer.

Good luck with that!

He sent me an easy smile. 'You wish for me to speak to her and explain. I can be very persuasive.'

Oh god.

I was actually dying inside now as I shook my head. 'That's not going to happen. Because I have no idea where she is—she may even be dead for all I know.'

He frowned. 'But still, this makes you unhappy. Because she would not approve?' he pressed me.

I huffed out an uneasy breath, feeling stupidly exposed again. And woefully gauche. The last thing he surely wanted right now was an in-depth analysis of my dysfunctional relationship with my mum, but it seemed he was not going to let it drop. And I had brought it up, so what choice did I have?

'On the contrary,' I mumbled, aware of him so close beside me. Suddenly I wished I could just give in to the desire racing through my body and forget about all my misgivings, but I knew I couldn't. *Quite.* 'She wouldn't disapprove. She'd probably think I'd hit the jackpot,' I said starting to feel nauseous. 'She was always so dependent on men,' I added, the shame engulfing me. As it had so often during my childhood. When she had turned up at the school gates with my newest 'new dad' who she'd picked up that afternoon. Or when I had gone into the living room in the morning and found her draped all over some random guy she'd brought home from the pub the night before.

I forced myself to look up, and gauge Renzo's reaction.

I was not sure what I had been expecting, probably disgust, or worst impatience—this conversation had to be a massive passion killer, right?—but what I saw instead was the sheen of something strong and vivid in his eyes, not sympathy exactly, but not boredom or irritation either, which surprised me enough to blurt out the rest.

'She collected men, boyfriends, hook-ups, any willing guy she met, really.' I shrugged. 'And she clung to them, until they got bored, and left her, because she was so needy, and insecure. And lonely, I suppose. Ever since my dad walked out on her.' And she always made sure to let me know, I was never going to be enough to fill that hole, I thought resentfully, but didn't add, because that would make this confessional even more excruciating.

I sighed, as a little of the panic and embarrassment released its hold on my throat. I had to tell Renzo the truth, even if it did make me look gauche and unsophisticated. I had no experience with these kind of relationships. With *any* sexual relationship really. And while I would hate for him to figure out he was the only guy I'd ever slept with, pretending to be someone I was not was somehow worse. Because that was what she had always done.

'I just…' I sucked in a breath and forced out the rest of it. 'I promised myself I'd never *ever* be like her.' I turned my face to his, but his expression had become strangely unreadable. 'And being your mistress, even for a little while, makes me feel as if I've somehow broken that promise to myself. Do you understand?'

CHAPTER TWELVE

Renzo

I STARED AT JESSIE, staggered not just by her honesty, but the way her story had affected me. First of all, I wanted to strangle her mother.

I imagined the men this woman had brought into Jessie's life. If they were anything like the men my mother had been forced to bring into mine... Those pigs, who had hurt and exploited her...and me.

The impotent fury I remembered from my childhood wrapped its tentacles around my chest, making it difficult to react for a moment.

I breathed through it, keeping my face carefully blank of the anger I felt—for Jessie, for myself, for my own mother—a trick I had learned as a boy.

Perhaps I should allow her to back out of our arrangement gracefully.

This 'liaison' was already more complicated than it was supposed to be. But as I sat there, forcing the tentacles to release their hold, I could feel the deep throbbing ache that only she had ever made me feel. And the spark of something else—admiration, affection, pride, protectiveness even—which I had never felt for another woman. And I knew I was not a decent man, so I would not do the decent thing.

I was far too selfish a man and a lover—and I wanted her too much—to be *that* altruistic.

But as the flush lit up her freckles, and her knuckles whitened on her adorable underwear, it occurred to me that maybe I could help her after all.

Jessie was hung up about sex. Why had I never realised this before? She had waited a long time to take a lover, being twenty when I had first slept with her. And I would hazard a guess she had had very few lovers since. Or she would not be so adorably artless and confused about our arrangement.

'But you do not *need* me, *Principessa*,' I murmured, even though I suspected she did, just not in the way she believed. 'You *want* me—these are two very different things, no?'

Her eyes widened, and the colour in her cheeks spread down to her collarbone.

The swell of excitement and exhilaration at the thought of helping her deal with her hang-ups, in the most pleasurable way possible, increased the ache in my groin, as I touched my thumb to her burning face, then trailed it down her neck, to the staggered rise and fall of her cleavage.

Her sharp intake of breath, the jolt of panic and aware-ness, told me all I needed to know.

Yes, she was scared of this connection. The intensity of our chemistry. This was not all that surprising, as it had scared me too, four years ago. But chemistry like this was so rare, it would be a sin to deny it.

'What we do together, in bed, is not about ownership,' I told her. 'It will not reduce your independence,' I said firmly. 'It will increase it. For you will no longer need to be afraid of your mother's legacy, or embarrassed by it. She is not here. It is only us two. And anything you give to me, I am committed to giving back to you, tenfold,' I said boldly, rel-ishing tonight, and the days and weeks ahead even more.

It seemed so obvious to me now that she had had few lovers since I had first initiated her. Why that should only make me feel more possessive of her, and excited at the prospect of unleashing her pleasure, and freeing her from the ghosts of her past, made no sense. But I did not intend to examine my reaction. The time for talk—for regrets—was over. She was unsure of herself, of her passion and desire—so I would have to show her how to own it.

It is a tough job, no. But I am more than up for it.

I swallowed the laugh which wanted to burst out of my mouth at the bad joke.

'Let me make love to you as you deserve, *Principessa*,' I coaxed, gliding my hands under the hem of her T-shirt, and gripping her waist to ease her off the bed, until she stood between my thighs, her body trembling under my hold, her gaze fixed on mine. 'Do you understand?' I asked, pushing her own words back at her.

Emotion shadowed her gaze, but I could see, she was already lost. Thoughts of her past, her mother, the promises she had made to herself that had no bearing on this moment were not relevant now, because she could deny me no longer.

She nodded.

Triumph surged, thickening my erection.

But I forced myself to hold back my groan, to ease off her T-shirt slowly, patiently. I would not devour her again. As I had last night. I had promised her a feast for the senses, and that was what I would deliver.

Even so, when I released her bra, and flung it away, I sucked in a sharp breath, to contain my vicious need at the tempting sight. She was so beautiful, so radiant—her breasts small but high and firm—her body lean but subtly curvy. And she was all mine, for the next three weeks.

All the compromises I had been forced to make would be worth it.

She trembled violently, as I caressed her yearning flesh, her hands landing on my shoulders, holding on to me, as if she needed my strength to stay upright. The sop to my damaged ego was nothing compared to the heat which fired through my veins as I stroked the puckered flesh and her nipples tightened and swelled. Her eyes—still a little wary—became dazed with desire. I kissed and suckled the hard tips, holding her steady, until she was gasping and shaking with need.

When I released her at last, I grinned at her, pressing one last kiss to her reddened nipple.

'I have always loved that you are so sensitive here,' I said, enjoying her even more, as the vivid colour fired across her chest again, and bloomed on her face.

'You remembered that?' she said, her astonishment impossibly endearing.

'Of course,' I said, realising there was nothing I did not recall from that night.

I would have been concerned at the deep pulse of emotion in my heart—a response to the innocence which still clung to her, despite everything—but I couldn't bring myself to feel anything but sheer joy. That she trusted me, in this much at least.

'Now, I intend to feast on the rest of you,' I murmured, the anticipation firing through me, as I stood and pressed her back onto the bed.

I kneaded my thigh absently, but the soreness there was overwhelmed by the ache in my groin.

I threw off my shirt, but chose to keep my erection in my pants for now, or I would be far too tempted to rush things...*again.*

I lifted one of her feet from the bed, and concentrated on untying her laces, my palms already beginning to sweat. Once her shoe was off, I ran my thumb down her instep and felt that gratifying shudder.

'Ticklish?' I teased, determined to lighten the mood. Somehow.

She shook her head, her gaze locked on mine. 'Turned on,' she replied, with that bold honesty which had always enchanted me.

The surge of longing became rich and fluid again. And painfully intense. The next twenty minutes—half an hour if I could last that long—were going to be pure torture. But I was determined to make this last.

I then set about taking off her other shoe, and sucking each of her toes, before easing off her jeans and working my way up her tempting calves, her trembling thighs. And I forced myself to concentrate on the growing ache in my groin, the glorious scent of her arousal, her live-wire responses and the brutal sensations skittering over my skin, so I could ignore the strange relentless ache which was also building in my heart.

CHAPTER THIRTEEN

Jessie

RENZO PARTED THE folds of my sex and licked the swollen flesh.

The orgasm which had been tantalising close as he teased and tortured every part of me—discovering erogenous zones I never knew I had—wound tighter inside me.

'Oh…please… Renzo.' I moaned, fisting my fingers in his hair, writhing against his devious mouth, reduced to begging.

I choked out a sob, the desire so raw now, I couldn't draw a decent breath.

Then he captured the throbbing nub of my clitoris and sucked. I arched up, bowed back, the sensations shattering in their intensity as my body gave itself over to the tidal wave of pleasure. At last.

He licked and sucked me through the last of the orgasm, and I was left, lying limp and shaking on the bed.

My body was sweaty with pleasure, my heart raw as I watched him strip off his jeans.

The mammoth erection jutted out. But the vicious pulse of renewed arousal faded as I noticed the terrible scarring on his left leg, the misshapen thigh, the torn flesh over his knee a testament to how much he had suffered. And how far he had come.

I lay on the bed unable to move or speak, the emotion choking me, as he pulled a foil pack out of his jeans pocket, and sheathed himself with clumsy fingers.

He glanced up to find me watching him. His eyes darkened, his gaze becoming hooded, as he climbed onto the bed. 'Don't look at that,' he said, his tone as raw as I felt.

My gaze glided over the other scars—the faded crudely drawn tattoos I remembered from that night—before it met his.

How could one man have endured so much pain? I wondered, the agonising emotion threatening to choke me, my eyes stinging.

His sensual lips quirked, but the smile was guarded. 'No pity, *Principessa*,' he murmured, and I remembered his mind-reading abilities from long ago too. 'I do not need it.'

It was not pity I felt, though, it was sadness, for the harsh life he must have led.

But before I could get the words out, he cradled my hips, and tugged me under him.

'This is all I want,' he insisted. Then he surged deep in one powerful thrust.

I groaned, the shattering fullness almost more than I could bear. But the ache in my chest was forgotten as I grabbed his shoulders, anchoring myself for his brutal possession as the pleasure charged back along my nerve endings.

He found a relentless rhythm—drawing out, pushing back—forcing me to take more of that hard length with each thrust, until I was impaled completely. But the pleasure never stopped building in fierce furious increments, taking me closer and closer to that tantalising, tormenting peak.

His groans matched my sobs, but then he shifted to glide his thumb over the tender nub.

The perfect touch triggered a tumultuous release, my sex massaging him as I soared over at last—and felt him fall into the abyss behind me.

But as I lay, sweaty and sated, and a little shaky from the force of my climax, the pain in my chest came charging back.

I slid my hands off his shoulders, and banded my arms around his big body, and I allowed myself the luxury of holding him as we both tumbled into sleep.

Renzo

'You have to hide, Ren, don't make a sound, no matter what happens... You must be a brave boy, then you must run.'

My mamma's terrified voice cuts through the darkness in rapid Italian. My heart is beating so loud, I'm scared the angry shouting voices will hear me. Clammy sweat sticks my torn T-shirt to my skin. The bed creaks above me, pushing down on my back, trapping me in the sweltering shadows. Heavy thuds, ugly grunts, muffled pops ricochet through my body. I can't move, I mustn't cry. Silent tears scald my cheeks making the skin burn—I taste metal in my mouth as I bite back the whimpers.

Then the burning pain in my lungs spreads to my leg, my heart beats faster, the heavy thuds turning to the clank and clatter of rending metal, and the medics shouting in French. But I can still hear my mamma's frantic whispers. And I am that boy again, trapped and gagging in a dark hole of his own terror.

I jerked away, the agonising cries for help caught in my

throat, as I was torn from the cruel dream and wrenched into reality.

Where am I?

Terror blindsided me. And I was too scared to move, still trapped under that bed—or was it the wreckage of my car?—my leg on fire, the darkness closing in around me.

I panted, struggling to draw breath, my body rigid, my mind dazed, my throat aching, my leg cramping… Then I caught the scent of roses, and the pain in my lungs eased.

'Renzo? What's wrong?'

Her voice was groggy with sleep, but thick with concern. Soft fingertips grazed my scarred cheek as her face appeared over mine in the moonlight. I leant into her palm, the rush of gratitude horrifying in its intensity as I was dragged the rest of the way out of the nightmare.

Fresh, salty air rippled over my skin and I wrapped my arms around her to pull her down, and roll her under me, so I could sink my face into her hair, gulp in a lungful of that clean, delicate scent. Tears stung my eyes… Tears of pain and loss and the bone-deep terror from my nightmares.

I found her mouth with mine and kissed her, fervent, desperate. She kissed me back with the same urgency. I caressed her sweet flesh, frantic and distraught, touching and teasing and tormenting all the places I knew would make her want me. At last, I delved between her thighs, the clamouring terror retreating further when I found the slick heat of her desire.

'I need to be inside you,' I stammered, hating the desperation in my voice, but not able to disguise it.

She nodded, and I angled her hips to plunge deep. She was tight, so tight, but she accepted me, clinging to me as I clung to her. The frantic passion built quickly, careering through me. I grunted, thrusting hard, pitifully grateful when I felt the spasm of her release. I yanked out just in time as my climax flooded my body and my seed spilled onto her belly.

Shame washed over me as I collapsed on top of her. I forced myself to roll off her, then dragged my aching body out of the bed.

'Renzo, where are you going?' she asked, confused now as well as concerned.

The last of the afterglow faded as I stumbled naked towards the terrace door.

'You will sleep better alone, *Principessa*,' I managed, my voice harsh even to my own ears. But I could not risk falling asleep in her arms again.

Not until I knew why the nightmares—which had haunted me during my boyhood and returned to torment me after the crash—had become more vivid, more disturbing. And why the only thing which could give me relief now from the searing terror was her...

CHAPTER FOURTEEN

Jessie

'*MADEMOISELLE JESSIE, il y a quatre femmes pour vous voir.*'

I glanced up from the croissant dough I was making for tomorrow's breakfast to find Eduardo in the doorway.

Four women were here to see me. How odd.

'*Qui sont-elles?*' I asked, frowning.

I was almost finished for the day, and was looking forward to dashing up to my room to change into my swimsuit, so I could join Renzo in our cove for a swim... Something he had suggested this morning before heading to his office in the chateau, for another series of meetings with his executives—something which had been keeping him busy as well as his physiotherapy while I worked for the past two weeks.

My face heated at the thought of all the things I had been anticipating doing to Renzo after our swim.

I cleared my throat, trying to contain my insta-blush.

No one cares what you are doing with Renzo after hours. Except you.

And the truth was, even I had become easier with our... *agreement*. Ever since that first night, when I had poured out all my fears about becoming my mum to Renzo—and he had made me realise, I didn't need to be afraid of her legacy. Not anymore.

Our sex-capades in the last two weeks had been nothing short of a revelation in that regard. Renzo had been more than happy to help me revel in my pleasure—*our* pleasure—until we were both shattered, then he would return to his own room.

I frowned.

Get over that. This is a casual fling, not a love affair. The fact Renzo has no desire to sleep in your bed after the sex is done, isn't important.

But I couldn't deny the twinge of disappointment, as I recalled the nightmare which had woken him up in my arms that first night. And the passionate, strangely tumultuous encounter which had followed.

There had been nothing like it since. Renzo's moves had become more seductive, more sophisticated and more skilled as each night had passed, and he dedicated himself to testing the limits of my pleasure—with patient determination—and brought me to orgasm… Over and over again…

But I couldn't seem to shake the memory of that nightmare, and the sounds he'd made before he woke—like an animal caught in a trap, terrified and frantic.

Eduardo shrugged. *'Je ne sais pas,'* he said, reminding me of my mysterious visitors, whose identity he had no clue about either. *'Mais elles ont apporté beaucoup de vêtements avec eux.'*

They had bought loads of clothes with them? *Huh*?

'Go, Jessie, I will finish these,' Matteo said, who'd arrived to do his evening shift half an hour early. The older chef—who had become a firm friend, and mentor, in the past two weeks—sent me a paternal smile and then nudged me aside to take over the croissant dough. 'You will like this surprise,' he finished with a bright smile.

'What surprise?' I asked. Was that why he had arrived so

early? I had heard him and Renzo chatting in Italian yesterday evening when he'd served our meal, but now I was feeling stupidly insecure.

I washed and dried my hands, brushing my palms on my apron.

'Go… And then you will find out,' Matteo added, still smiling.

Clearly, he knew who these women were, because Renzo must have told him. Last night. Without telling me.

It was nice of Renzo to bother going to the trouble of surprising me. But even so, I was wary and tense as I headed up to my suite, where Eduardo had told me the women were waiting. I didn't like surprises, probably because so many of the surprises in my life before now had not been good ones.

What about Belle turning up on your doorstep pregnant with Cai all those years ago?

The thought popped into my head, and I held on to it, as I walked into the suite.

A middle-aged woman, exquisitely dressed in a designer pants suit, stood in the centre of the sitting room, surrounded by rails of clothing and flanked by three other women—one of whom seemed to be her assistant. The other two wore tailored white labcoats as they arranged an array of cases filled with make-up and perfumes next to a very professional looking salon chair which had appeared as if by magic.

I had never felt more underdressed in my life, wearing my standard kitchen uniform of flour-stained T-shirt and worn jeans. *'Bonjour,'* I managed.

All four women turned in unison, then the ringleader strolled towards me on ice-pick heels with a warm smile lighting her dark eyes.

'Mademoiselle Burton. A pleasure,' she replied in accented but perfect English as she gripped my hand. Her gaze roamed over me. 'You are perfect,' she said as approval twinkled in the deep brown. 'Monsieur Camaro told me you were exquisite. He did not lie.'

Monsieur Camaro said what now?

I tugged my fingers out of her grasp, starting to panic.

'I'm sorry, I didn't catch your name?'

'I am Madame Lavigne, stylist to the stars,' she said with a humorous flourish.

She folded her arm through mine to draw me into the room and introduced me to the other women, which included her assistant, Sophie, a renowned hairstylist called Natalie Dupont and a top make-up artist called Farah Amin.

'But you must call me Amal, Jessie,' Madame Lavigne murmured as her assistant started to take my measurements. 'You must not be concerned.' Amal's smile became sympathetic, as I stood dumbly, so out of my depth I was drowning. 'We have only five days to finish your look for the Allegri Ball in Monaco. But we will make you a vision, I guarantee it.'

The panic knotted around my throat. 'Okay,' I said, but I felt anything but okay.

The ball I had once been so excited about was only a week away.

Our time together was nearly over. In a week, I would have to leave the chateau. And Renzo.

There would be no more nights of liberating pleasure, no more sunset swims in our secret cove, no more days spent seeing him become more and more engaged in his business, no more chances to see Renzo devouring my food as he joked with me about my skills in the kitchen being almost as good as my skills in his bed...

And there would be no more opportunities to finally ask

him all those questions that had been queuing up in my head... About the man who took my virginity, who got me pregnant, who fathered the baby I lost, but who was still an enigma in so many ways.

Should I tell him about the pregnancy? The miscarriage?

Over the last few weeks, I'd begun to question my decision to bury the truth inside me. He wasn't the man I had met four years ago anymore. Plus my feelings for him had become so much deeper, and more complex, not just as we tore each other's clothes off each night, but during all those magic stolen moments during the day too.

But as the highly professional Amal and her team got to work putting together my 'look' for the Allegri event, I realised Renzo hadn't forgotten, or wilfully ignored our approaching end date, the way I had. By hiring Amal Lavigne, he was fulfilling his end of our bargain. Which had to mean, he was ready to let me go...

How could I tell him about the miscarriage now? Without looking manipulative... Or worse, needy? And how could I ask him all the questions that still tormented me, about his nightmare, and the reckless playboy who had discarded me so easily...

As the stylist and her team measured me, and prodded at me, chatting about the marvellous society debut that awaited me in Monaco, my heart sank into my toes. I didn't object to any of it, and an hour later, after they had left and Renzo appeared looking sheepish, I pretended that I was still excited about the ball, and that I was happy to accept the beyond generous new wardrobe so I wouldn't feel out of place at the event.

But as he made fierce passionate love to me that night, forcing me to three brutal orgasms before finding his own release, and then left the room while he thought I was sleeping, my heart swelled painfully in my throat and tears scalded the back of my eyes.

Our affair would be over in five days' time, and I refused to risk ruining the short time we had left together with anything deep or heavy. But that meant burying the pain and the truth about the miscarriage back inside me again—which had been threatening to spill out for weeks now without me even realising it. But far worse, it meant pretending I hadn't fallen hopelessly in love with the man that reckless playboy had become.

CHAPTER FIFTEEN

Five days later... In Monaco

Renzo

MY BREATH GOT trapped in my lungs and the familiar heat pooled in my groin as I stood in the doorway to Jessie's adjoining suite on the upper floors of Dante Allegri's Inferno Casino.

We had arrived in Monaco that afternoon on the Destiny Inc helicopter, and I had been ushered out of her suite two hours ago, so that the stylist and her crew could prepare Jessie. But I had heard them finally leave moments ago.

I watched as Jessie stared at her reflection in the mirror, now, unaware of my presence.

She was dressed in a stunning off-the-shoulder red satin gown, which hugged her subtle curves like a second skin and pushed up her breasts, making her cleavage a work of art.

My ribs tightened, making my thundering heartbeat almost deafening.

I still wasn't sure what had possessed me to describe the dress I wanted Jessie to wear to Lavigne in detail when I had hired her. But I could not deny the staggering effect it was having on me now.

This gown was more expensive, the material bolder and more luxurious, than the one Jessie had worn all those years ago. But the effect on me was exactly the same. I was mesmerised, enchanted, spellbound with lust and something else, something I had struggled to control for days now—weeks even—damn it.

As always, I attempted to concentrate on the lust—and discard that desperate emotion which had begun to haunt me, tormenting me each night as the nightmares returned when I was in my self-imposed exile, and I had to force myself not to return to her bed, to wake her and plunge into her again.

But somehow my desire—like my nightmares—and the inexplicable decision to make her wear *that* dress for me again were all equally problematic.

Why had the connection we had shared since that night only become more intense, more desperate, more insatiable in the past three weeks, no matter how many times I took her?

Perhaps it was simply that each time I touched her, tempted her, each time I tortured us both—drawing out her pleasure simply to prove that I could—her artless response to me had only become braver, bolder and more honest, and all the more intoxicating for it.

Making me greedy for every second of her company.

I didn't want to take her to the event upstairs which had already begun in the Inferno's palatial roof garden. The thought of having to socialise with anyone, when I only had one more night with her, tortured me now, as it had been torturing me for days.

How can I let her go? When I'm not ready to lose her. And why should I?

My palms started to sweat, my breathing becoming ragged.

I licked my lips, the elaborate chignon the stylist had spent hours constructing revealing the graceful line of her neck, the soft skin of her nape to my hungry gaze. Desire surged in my groin because I knew now exactly how much she loved to be kissed there.

I sunk my fists into my trouser pockets and forced myself to clear my throat rather than charge across the room.

Jessie's gaze connected with mine in the mirror. For a moment I could see a flicker of panic—followed by awareness—in the pale silvery blue. And I was reminded painfully of the girl who had once informed me with such artless candour I was to be her first lover.

'Bonsoir, Principessa,' I murmured as I crossed the silk carpet, my tone so husky the words scraped my throat. 'Madame Lavigne is worth her exorbitant price I see,' I added, trying to sound sophisticated when all my baser instincts were already in free fall.

Her gaze remained riveted to mine. Did she feel it too? This urgency? This desperation? Surely, she must? How could she be ready to let me go either? Three weeks hadn't been long enough, that had to be obvious to her too.

I had waited, I realised, for days now, weeks even, as I brought her to staggering pleasure each night for her to ask for more. But she hadn't, and now our time was nearly over…

Her cheeks flushed the dark vermilion I had come to adore as I reached her.

'Renzo, this dress…' she said, chewing her bottom lip in a way which had the need surging again in my gut. But the fierce emotion in her face made my heart throb into my throat. What was it I could see in her eyes? Surprise and confusion I could understand—I was not even sure myself why I had been so determined to see her again as she had been that night, fresh and forthright and only mine—but there was something else there that made no sense, because it looked strangely like guilt.

'It's just like the one I wore that night,' she added, as if she believed the similarity had been an accident.

'I know, I asked Madame Lavigne to recreate it. I wanted to see you in it again,' I managed, realising that a part of me had always wanted desperately to be able to go back to that night and be a better man than I had been then.

Stupid to realise that now, I thought. After I had been insisting to myself for so long that all I had ever really wanted out of our liaison was to become that man again.

'But...why?' she asked, looking more confused, more wary, even as the emotion deepened the pale blue of her irises. The searching light in her eyes though—as if she were looking for something—terrified me.

'Because I want you now, even more than I did then,' I murmured, grasping her wrist and dragging her into my arms, still desperate to convince myself my need was all about sex. 'Undress. Or I will rip it,' I said, my voice harsh with the demand I didn't want to control anymore, because it was a good way to hide all the other emotions churning inside me.

Not just need but longing, and the fear of losing her a second time. The fear of the intimacy which had snuck up on me in the past weeks and months and was making it impossible now for me to even contemplate letting her go.

Jessie's eyes widened, but I could see the flare of arousal, behind the flicker of shock. I was behaving like a caveman, the skill and sophistication I had tried so hard to show her over the last three weeks burning to ash in my mouth. But what concerned me more was the way the searching light in her eyes had died.

What had she been looking for? And why did it hurt now to think that I might be incapable of giving it to her?

I swallowed heavily, as she stepped back, and found the tab underneath her arm, to draw the zip down.

Suddenly I was thrown back to that night so long ago, when I had made her strip for me. But that man—the one who could be patient, provocative, who could deny the emotional hold she now had over me—no longer existed.

What shocked me though was the realisation that I didn't want him to return. Not anymore. Not if it meant I could not have her.

The gown dropped to pool at her feet in a waterfall of heavy red satin. She was barefoot, her lacy underwear the type I would once have found alluring, seductive. But as I gulped—trying to moisten the parched feeling in my throat—and grasped her upper arm to drag her back into my embrace, to make her aware of the heavy erection pressing against my tuxedo trousers, this didn't feel like a seduction, it felt like a wildfire.

'I need you, now, *Principessa*,' I groaned as I pressed my face into her neck, and covered her lace-covered breast with one urgent hand, to plump and pluck the taut flesh.

She nodded, as she flung her arms around my neck.

'Yes, Renzo, I know,' she said, her voice as raw as mine.

I fastened my lips on the pulse point hammering in her throat, then drew my hand down the trembling line of her body and slid my fingers into the lace panties.

She was soaking wet for me already. But even as my hunger rejoiced, my heart rebounded in my chest. And the fear strangled me. I couldn't let her go. And I wouldn't.

I turned her, the need surging so heavily in my groin, I

felt frantic, desperate, to mark her, to brand her, to make her mine…

For good this time…

I struggled to dismiss the scary thought, as I swept the debris off an occasional table. She gasped as a vase and her clutch purse crashed to the floor.

'Renzo?' she said, as I bent her over the table with one hand on her back, while I released the thick erection from my trousers with the other.

'It's okay, I'll be gentle,' I said, to reassure, even though I didn't know if I could be.

'I don't need you to be,' she said, making the need surge harder, faster.

I grappled with the condom, cursing viciously under my breath, ripped off the lace covering her bottom. Her thighs quivered, and I knew from her whimper she was waiting for me, ready for me.

At last, I clamped shaking hands on her bare hips, and plunged into her to the hilt from behind. She sobbed, tightening around my length, as I worked the spot I knew would make her come—hard, fast, desperate.

Only a few moments later, the orgasm slammed into me even as she massaged me, climaxing with me, her cries echoing with my guttural shouts.

For one hideous moment I felt brutally ashamed. I had taken as if she were…

A whore.

The ugly word hissed in my consciousness but was swept away by the searing wave of afterglow.

I collapsed over her, making the table wobble precariously. Even as my knees weakened from the force of my climax, I managed to brace my hand against the table, felt the strength in both my legs as I drew out of her.

I dragged her up, turned her around in my arms. And clasped her to me as I somehow managed to get us both to the nearest couch. We sunk onto it together in a sweaty mess.

Her carefully constructed hairdo had been ruined, her perfectly applied make-up was smudged. The beautiful red dress was a heap of crushed satin on the floor. My shirt was creased, my trousers still undone. But as the afterglow continued to fire through my veins, I stripped off the condom, adjusted my trousers, then cradled her naked body in my arms and brushed the sweaty tendrils of hair off her brow.

I wasn't sad, or ashamed—I was utterly content.

Because I knew, tonight wasn't the end now. It couldn't be. Why did I have to let her go? *Why*? When everything was so good between us.

'Madame Lavigne is going to kill us if she ever finds out what we've just done' she said.

I laughed. I couldn't help it, her pragmatism, and her concern at how the stylist would react to having her hard work destroyed as adorable as everything else about her. I grinned down at her. 'I will repair the damage.'

'Last time I looked, you weren't an award-winning hairstylist,' she murmured.

I cupped her cheek, adoring the flushed indignation on her face even more.

'I have created a new style for you,' I said, letting my gaze roam over the chestnut curls rioting around her face in glorious disarray. 'Called the Well Loved Look.'

Her eyes widened, the sudden sheen of hope and emotion so devastating it wrenched at my soul.

I basked in that look for several giddy, golden moments as I realised what I had said, and that I had no urge to take the words back. It felt good, to finally tell the truth. Not just to her, but also to myself.

And it made me realise that the answer to my panic, my confusion, my fears—over the last few days and weeks—had been there all along.

I loved Jessie. And she loved me.

'I want you to stay with me, Jessie,' I said, finally saying what I had wanted to say to her for weeks.

'I…' She blinked, several times, but the sheen of emotion in her eyes became guarded. 'Let me think about it.'

I could not see what there was to think about. But I said nothing more as she scrambled out of my arms. Clearly she needed time to adjust to my momentous revelation.

'I should go and take a shower. We're late for the ball.' She rushed over to pick up the broken shards of the vase, tidied away the other debris, still naked but for her bra and the torn panties, still glowing from our tryst. Still utterly adorable. 'I'll call Natalie, ask her to repair the hairdo then I should…' She continued to babble about the practicalities of rehiring the stylist, getting the dress pressed and arriving at the ball before everyone realised we were missing, as she picked up the dress, folded it over her arm, then fled towards her bathroom.

I didn't respond to any of it. I simply sat, sated, satisfied, stupidly pleased—with my revelation. And her reaction to it.

She was nervous, probably still in shock after the intensity of our love-making and my surprise declaration. But it was all good, I decided, as I heard the shower go on and finally managed to rouse myself from the couch, and dispose of the condom properly.

Once we got back from the ball, I would explain how we were going to proceed. That I did not want to lose her. That we were a couple now and I loved her. That this was not the end—it was a beginning.

The golden glow spreading through me became turbocharged, as I headed towards my own suite to get ready for a ball I was much more happy to attend now.

Because my time with Jessie would no longer end tonight.

CHAPTER SIXTEEN

Jessie

'JESS, YOU LOOK absolutely stunning. I can't believe you're here as Renzo's date. Or that you didn't tell me you two had become an item.' Belle sent me a sweet smile, then wiggled her eyebrows at me, her expression full of excitement for me and my surprise date.

The guilty blush fired over my skin. I should have told Belle what was going on weeks ago. But my guilt over that was nothing compared to the turmoil of emotions which had been turning my insides to mush ever since I had seen the dress Renzo had had designed for me. Which had only got worse when he had made frantic, passionate love to me in my suite. And then…

'I have created a new style for you, called the Well Loved Look.'

Those words had made me euphoric, because I could see the approval in his eyes. Hope had burst inside me, and for one blissful second, I had believed Renzo and I could have a future together.

But when he had added, only moments later that he wanted me to stay with him, reality had come crashing down on me.

How could we have a future, when we had never really

faced our past? When he still didn't know about the pregnancy I had lost. I loved Renzo, and I was sure, in his own way, he loved me. But I didn't feel secure with him. How could I be sure he wouldn't leave me, the way he had that morning so long ago, if I couldn't even get up the guts to tell him how much he had hurt me once?

Even since we had arrived at the ball, my fear and confusion had only become more acute. Because this glitzy, glittering crowd, this lavish luxurious event had once been part of Renzo's old life—a life he had stepped back into seamlessly as soon as we had arrived—but it had never been a part of mine.

The ballroom was on the top floor of the Belle Epoque palace which housed Dante Allegri's famous casino the Inferno. Iron filigree balconies ran the length of the building, looking out onto the bay where moonlight glittered on the array of huge superyachts moored in the dock, and the lights of billion-dollar mansions dotted the coastline. A large marble staircase in the middle of the space led up to the stunning roof garden, where Belle and I now stood, complete with fountains and exotic plants, and lit by glowing torchlight. The beautiful people who surrounded us were either gorging themselves on cordon bleu cuisine and vintage champagne or dancing to an A-list rock band in the ballroom below—who usually filled out football stadiums.

Renzo had introduced me to the Italian billionaire Dante Allegri and his beautiful wife, Edie, earlier, but all I could think about as we met them was that they might be able to see my hair was not as perfect as it should have been, that my dress was still a little crushed, that my make-up had been hastily applied.

'He looks so well, Jessie. Like his old self, but better,' Belle murmured, the thoughtful observation only making the turmoil in my stomach worse. 'You're obviously good for each other.'

'Do you really think so?' I murmured, trying desperately to quell my growing anxiety—and control all the insecurities which had always been there, but which I had never really acknowledged until now.

'Of course.' Belle sent me a puzzled frown. 'What's wrong, Jessie?' she asked, her gaze full of concern, because she had always been able to read me so easily.

'He wants me to stay with him, Belle, but I don't know if I can.' I forced the words out, as my gaze landed on Renzo on the other side of the roof garden talking to Dante and Alexi—and the yearning, the longing, swelled in that empty space in the pit of my stomach, which only he had ever been able to fill.

Light gleamed off his dark hair, and his tall frame in the tailored tuxedo reminded me of the man I had first met—but even though I knew he was so much more vivid and intense now than that reckless playboy, the panic still clawed at my throat.

Renzo glanced around, almost as if he could feel my eyes on him. Our gazes connected and the familiar burst of heat surged through me as his lips curved in that devastating smile. But the sharp, cruel yank in my chest—caused by the truth I had never been able to admit to him—only become more vicious.

'Why can't you? When it's so obvious you love him,' Belle said, so simply, I felt tears sting my eyes.

I forced my gaze away from Renzo, the panic making my fingers tremble on the champagne flute in my hand. 'Because it was him, Belle,' I whispered.

'Him who?' she said, confused.

'He was the father of the baby I lost,' I said, the need to

finally tell someone the whole sad, miserable story unstoppable. 'I stole your invite, went to his masquerade ball that night in Paris. He was my first lover. And the next morning he was just gone. I couldn't contact him. He didn't want to know.' A tear streaked down my face, as Belle grabbed my hand, and squeezed my fingers.

'Oh Jessie, I'm so so sorry that happened to you. He shouldn't have done that. But what did he say when you told him?' she asked, as she took the champagne glass out of my hand and passed it to a waiter. 'Surely he must have apologised.' She wiped the single tear away gently with her thumb. 'I can't believe he wouldn't want to make amends now, because it's obvious he adores you too.'

I blinked, as the emotions which had been so close to the surface all evening threatened to strangle me. 'I haven't told him about the pregnancy, the miscarriage.'

'Why not?' she asked, her thumb rubbing across my trembling knuckles, as she attempted to soothe the raw emotions making my hands shake.

'Because if I do, it will bring it all back,' I said.

How could I have believed that seeing Renzo again, that falling in love with him, wouldn't make that part of our past real again too?

'And I don't know how he will react,' I managed, scared now at the thought of how much power he had over me already. 'I thought I'd got over it.' The words rushed out of me like a flood. 'That it didn't matter. But it does. And now it's too late to tell him. I should have told him sooner. He loves an illusion. He loves the woman he met that night. But I'm not her anymore.'

'Shh, shh, Jessie, you're panicking,' Belle said. Then she pulled me into her arms and held me tight, as the guests around us began to stare. 'You don't know how he will react until you tell him,' she whispered in my ear. 'By the way, he's heading over here because he can see you're distressed,' she added. 'Surely that has to be a good sign.'

I pulled out of her arms, to see Renzo striding towards us.

The panic consumed me. I couldn't tell him, not here, not like this. Maybe not ever, because then I would be totally exposed.

'I have to go,' I said to Belle, and before she could say more, I turned and rushed towards the exit. The soft glimmer of the torchlight blinded me and made the tears I couldn't shed scald my eyes. As I pushed through the crowd of beautiful people, the subtle scent of expensive perfumes and colognes suffocated me.

I had to get away. I couldn't stay here. I didn't belong, any more than I belonged in Renzo's life. And I could see now I never had. I thought we were both damaged, both equal, but I'd never been able to share my pain with him, and now I knew why. Because I was scared of becoming my mother still. Scared of needing him too much. Scared of the power he would have to hurt me if I allowed myself to trust him. To love him. All the way.

Renzo

I watched Jessie dash through the crowd, the sick feeling in my stomach starting to churn.

Something was wrong. But what?

Once I finally reached Belle, I glared at her. Had she said something to upset Jessie? But I could see she looked shell-shocked too.

'What's going on?' I demanded, unable to keep the accusation out of my voice. I'd known ever since we'd arrived at the ball Jessie was nervous—I had convinced myself it had to be because she wasn't used to these kind of expensive, superficial society events, which were all pomp and circumstance, but had no real value.

I'd been determined to put her at her ease, which was why I had forced myself to leave her with her cousin—because my presence only seemed to be putting her more on edge. But even so, I hadn't been able to take my eyes off her. And when I'd seen Belle pull her into a hug, her body language so stiff and shaky, my uneasiness had gone into overdrive.

'What were you talking about?' I asked, struggling to control my panic now, and the sick feeling in my gut. 'And where is she going?' I demanded, the thought that she might be leaving me something I refused to even contemplate, but something that had taken ahold of me as I'd followed her frantic dash through the crowd.

'Stop talking to my wife in that tone of voice.'

I turned to see Galanti bearing down on me with a furious frown on his face. Before I had a chance to tell him to go to hell though, Belle intervened.

'It's okay, Alexi,' she said, her voice calming, before she grasped my arm.

The look on her face—concerned, worried and full of compassion—made the panic become turbocharged. And a thousand recriminations fired through my mind.

Why had I brought Jessie here? Why had I insisted on coming to this ball? Why hadn't I demanded an answer from her earlier? Why hadn't I told her properly I loved her?

I clenched my fists, but even as I struggled to control my panic, I felt broken inside, the way I had when she had first walked back into my life... The way I had felt, in truth, long before the crash. The way I had felt as a boy, when I couldn't protect my mother. And the way I had felt every night in the past weeks when I had woken from those horrendous nightmares, shaky, terrified, alone, and Jessie had not been by my side.

'Renzo, you need to go after her,' Belle said, her voice gentle but forceful. 'There's something she needs to tell you…'

The comment was cryptic enough to be maddening, but I could see from the sheen in Belle's eyes she was being loyal to her cousin. Whatever this was, it was not her secret to tell.

I swore and charged after Jessie, but as I shoved through the throng of guests—people I had once been so determined to impress, but who I cared nothing about anymore—my leg began to ache, while the panic wrapped around my chest and threatened to crack my ribs.

CHAPTER SEVENTEEN

Jessie

I DASHED ALONG the corridor, towards the lavish adjoining suites we shared at the casino.

The fact that Renzo had requested adjoining suites only spurred my determination to run, as soon as I could get out of this dress, as I scrabbled around for the key card.

But then I heard uneven footsteps thudding on the carpeting behind me.

I turned, and saw Renzo approaching, his face determined... His expression concerned.

My insides knotted with nerves and my heartbeat thumped against my ribs like gunfire.

'Jessie, where are you going?' he asked, his voice gruff with concern and confusion.

As he reached me, he pressed a palm to my burning cheek.

A dozen different lies to explain my disappearing act raced through my brain, but got caught in my throat when he said, 'Belle said you had something you needed to tell me.'

His voice was soft and persuasive, but also raw.

I wanted to hate Belle. How could she have betrayed me, but even as I tried to blame her, I knew I couldn't. This was a mess of my own making.

I shook my head, stared down at my hands. My knuckles had whitened as I clutched the key card. The truth locked inside me still.

He took the card out of my numb fingers, cupped my elbow, then slid the key card through the lock and shoved the door open to draw me into the suite.

The moonlight shone off the luxury antique furniture—the glitter of light outside outlined the view of the bay. He didn't let go of my hand though as he threw the card on the table. The same table where we had made love so frantically less than two hours ago.

I began to shake as he led me towards the suite's balcony, his limp barely noticeable now. He tucked a knuckle under my chin, raised my face. His gaze searched for the answer I didn't want to give him, because it would leave me so exposed. But when I saw the grim determination in his eyes, I knew my time was up. I couldn't lie, couldn't hide any longer.

But the air got trapped in my lungs.

'Breathe, *Principessa*,' he said gently.

Something about that regal endearment, which reminded me so much of the man he used to be, the man I had trusted when I shouldn't have, had the air bursting out.

I gulped down another breath, trying to ease the burning in my chest, the stinging sensation in my eyes from the tears I had held in for what felt like a lifetime.

'Whatever it is,' he said, 'I want to know.'

I blinked furiously, but the tears slipped over my lids. He brushed them away with his thumbs.

'I… I got pregnant,' I said. 'That night.'

'*Che cosa?*' His hands dropped from my face, his eyes widening in shock. Then his gaze jerked to my stomach. '*Mio bambino?* You had my baby?'

I shook my head, struggling to find the right words. But it had always been a baby to me, I realised now. Even though it had only lived for a few short months inside me.

'I had a miscarriage,' I managed, swallowing around the pain that would always remain in some hidden corner of my heart.

'You did not tell me this? Why did you not?' he asked, his voice so raw now it was barely audible, but all I could hear was the slice of accusation. The reaction I had feared.

'I tried to tell you, when I found out, but I didn't have your number... And none of your employees would put me through to...'

'Not then,' he cut me off, his eyes darkening. '*Now*. Why did you not tell me *now*? When I discovered who you were? When we made love, so many times? When I asked you to stay with me? Why did you not tell me *anytime over the last few weeks*?'

His voice wasn't soft anymore, but the slice of anger was doing nothing to disguise the hurt in his eyes.

I pulled away from him, folded my hands around my waist, the crippling pain turning to agony. But something about his anger, made me angry too.

He was asking me a question I hadn't had an answer for. Until now.

'Because it was *my* loss. Not yours,' I said, feeling that hollow pain becoming a chasm. 'Because I wanted to have the baby and you never even knew it existed.'

'Because you kept it from me,' he said, but his voice broke on the words.

'You left me without a word the next day,' I said, my anger building to disguise the pain. 'I tried over and over to contact you and you didn't respond. And then I got a text from one of your minions offering me fifty thousand

euro to go away. And two days later, the bleeding started.'
I gulped, the tears flowing freely now. 'It hurt, so much.
But what hurt more was realising I wanted you there with
me, and I didn't even know you. I felt abandoned, the way
I had when my mother had left me. But just like her, I was
clinging to something that had never existed. Wanting the
support of someone who didn't want me.' The anguish of
those days in the hospital which had been trapped inside
me made the words queue up too quickly in my throat and
then spew out in a rush. 'I couldn't be that vulnerable again.
So I convinced myself it was okay, that it hadn't been that
bad. That I hadn't needed you. But I had. And when we got
back together, I had to keep on lying to myself. And then...'
I panted, trying to get the words out now so he would see
and understand. But I could already see the anger in his
eyes had died. 'And then today you told me you wanted
me to stay with you. And for a moment I was so happy.
But then I knew it couldn't be real. That it wasn't enough.
You won't even sleep the whole night in the same bed as
me, Renzo. I don't know much more about you now than
I did back then. And I'm still too scared to ask. How can
that be love? Really? When you don't trust me any more
than I trust you?'

'Stop...' He clasped my face, dragged me into his body
and wrapped his arms around me. The shuddering pain
wracked me. 'I'm sorry. I'm sorry,' he murmured, stroking
my hair, holding me so tightly I could hear his heart beating
against my ear. 'You are right, I did not check the condom. I
should have checked it. But you were... So much. Too much.
You were always different from the other women, Jessie.
Even then. I left you that morning because I was terrified
of the feelings I had for you.'

The wrenching sobs burst from my mouth—the dam

of emotions breaking inside me. Suddenly I was pressed against him, my body wracked with the misery of losing our baby all over again. But this time I wasn't alone. He was with me.

Tentatively, haltingly, I banded my arms around his back, and clung to him, to keep myself upright, to calm the sobs to pants. And accepted his comfort at last.

Eventually, I shuddered to a stop. I was aware of the soreness in my ribs, the feel of his dress shirt damp against my cheek. But the pain in my heart, which would always be there, felt different now, less raw, less cruel, less lonely.

He dragged my head back, cupped my cheeks to lift my face to his.

'I am so sorry, Jessie. I failed you, as I failed her.'

The agony in his face was so vivid it shocked me out of the last of my crying jag. His eyes were shadowed with guilt and a bone-deep terror. Reminding me of the man who had cried out in his sleep all those weeks ago. The man who I suspected had been chased by the same nightmare in the weeks since, but who I had been sure would never confide in me.

Our problems had never just been about the miscarriage, I realised.

I'd been so terrified to admit I wanted more from him, from this relationship. That when he'd finally offered it, I hadn't trusted he meant it. But now I could see, this wasn't just on him, and the mistakes he'd made in the past, but also on me, for never having the guts to ask all those questions because I'd convinced myself he wouldn't answer them.

So I forced myself to cradle his cheek, I finally let him see all the love in my heart and I took that final leap too.

'Who did you fail, Renzo? Is she the woman you have nightmares about?'

Renzo

I leant into Jessie's palm, trying to control the terrifying fear of losing her.

My insides felt as if they had been turned inside out already—at hearing of the pain she had endured, alone, because of my carelessness, my cowardice.

I didn't want to answer her question. Because then she would know how little I had to offer. But the way she had asked the question—so direct, so artless, so honest, as always—made me realise I no longer had a choice. How could I ever atone for the pain I had caused her, how could she ever trust me, if I could not tell her the truth of my past?

I could not look into her eyes though, while I did it. So I stepped back. The warm weight of her hand dropped from my face and I felt the loss instantly. I thrust my fists into my pockets and looked out at the night.

Luxury yachts bobbed in the marina below us, the headlamps of expensive cars wound through the hillside, past the mansions and chateaux of the superrich... But all I could see in that moment was the squalid room in the small-town brothel in Puglia where I had lived as a child. The place I had run away from as a boy, but had never really been able to escape. Because it had always been there in my nightmares. The ugly sound of sex, bought and paid for, the sickly smell of cheap perfumes and sweat and the suffocating desperation of the women trapped inside.

'My mother,' I murmured. 'My mother is the woman I failed. Just as I failed you.'

'You weren't the only one who failed, Renzo. I failed you too, by not telling you about the miscarriage a lot sooner,' she said with far too much generosity. Her hand settled on my back, rubbing, soothing, drawing me back to the present, and giving me the courage to confront my ugly past. 'Why do you think you failed her?'

Think? There it was again, her determination to always see the best in me. Despite all the evidence to the contrary. I hadn't just failed her. I swallowed, my throat raw. I had failed our baby too. I hated myself, imagining what might have happened if I had responded to her attempts to reach me. Would I have been ready to become a father? Certainly not. The thought would surely have terrified me. But the thought of what we had lost was compounded now by the realisation that fathering a child with her wouldn't terrify me anymore. It would make me so happy.

'I do not think, I *know*,' I said. 'My mother was forced to become *una prostitute*.' I spat the word out, because it had always disgusted me, in any language. It was not who she was, but what she had been forced to do. 'Because of me.'

'How could it be because of you?' she asked simply.

'Because I asked constantly for the things the other children had. I wanted money, respect. I hated to wear other children's cast off clothes, but this was all she could afford with the money she made as a waitress.' I shrugged, the bitterness in my voice doing nothing to hide the guilt. 'The town was controlled by the Brotherhood—a criminal gang. She took out loans she could not afford to pay for the things I wanted. She was still young, still pretty and this is the way they made her pay her debt.'

'What happened to her?' Jessie asked softly.

'She died, they killed her—because they found out she planned to leave with me. The nightmares take me back to that night when I was twelve and I hid under the bed while they hurt her. And I did nothing to save her. She told me to run, so I did. And I kept on running.'

I hung my head, my breathing ragged. Now Jessie knew

the shame of who I really was. Tears burnt my eyes—how could she ever care for a man like me?

'For years, as I made my fortune, as I became wealthy, desired, I thought I had escaped.' I shook my head. 'But then you came into my life and you terrified me. Because for the first time, I wanted more. The crash made me realise I deserved to be punished. Then you came back… And…' I turned, forcing myself to look at her. She stood behind me, her face a picture of sadness. I didn't understand it. where was the disgust I had expected and deserved? 'I used you, the way I used so many women, *Principessa*,' I said simply, the endearment like acid on my tongue, because it reminded me of that reckless playboy. The man who had used sex and persuasion, flattery and money, and had believed that would be enough to win a woman like her. 'But with you it was *always* different. I hope you can believe me.'

I was suddenly exhausted, the emotions swirling in my stomach, my breath trapped in my lungs, my throat burning. 'You must know, the baby died inside you, because it was mine.'

'Oh Renzo…' She shook her head, and another tear fell. She swiped it away with her fist. Then to my utter shock, she stepped to me, wrapped her arms around my waist. And pressed her cheek to my chest 'That's nonsense,' she said, the determination I adored thick in her voice. 'Just like it's nonsense that you were to blame for your mother's death.'

She lifted her face to mine, the faith in her eyes soothing the painful memories—and alleviating some of the paralysing guilt. 'Or I was to blame for my mother deserting me.'

I placed my hands on her shoulders. If I were a better man, I would push her away. But I couldn't do anything but draw her closer—and absorb her forgiveness. Her understanding. I wasn't convinced I deserved her, but I knew I was far too selfish a man to ever let her go.

She tightened her hold, then she blindsided me again. 'I love you, Renzo. And I would love to stay with you.'

I leant down to press my face into her fragrant curls, so overcome I couldn't speak.

I could feel the soft swell of her breasts flatten against me. And the desire to take her to bed, to lose myself in her again…and again…and again…was so fierce, so powerful, so all-consuming, the blood surged into my groin. But the giddy desire was nothing compared to the soaring emotion lifting my heart into my throat.

I nodded, fiercely, then lifted her face to press kisses to her cheeks, her throat, her forehead. *'Ti amo, cara,'* I said, my English having deserted me entirely.

A bright smile spread across her face and burst in my heart. 'I'm hoping that means what I think it means,' she said with a chuckle.

I lifted her into my arms, to spin her around, delighted by her laughter.

There would be struggles ahead, I knew this. We were both bruised and battered souls, defensive and scared to trust because of our pasts. But as I allowed myself to bask in her love, I knew I would do everything in my power to earn her trust. To deserve her. Forever.

As I placed her back on her feet, I could wait no longer to capture her lips—and brand her as mine. She kissed me back with equal fervour, the sweet sobs of her surrender firing my need.

But as we undressed frantically, and fell onto her bed together—the urgent touches and fierce kisses unleashing the reckless passion which had always been a part of our relationship—I was already anticipating the riches she would bring into my life.

And as I thrust into her at last, and she welcomed me into the tight sweet clasp of her body, I knew I could not wait to start unwrapping every single one.

EPILOGUE

Renzo

'YOU ARE THE most beautiful little girl who has ever lived, *mia piccola principessa Giorgia*.' I grinned down at the tiny baby in my arms, who was staring back at me with her mother's blue eyes, and breathed in the precious scent I had come to adore of baby powder, sour milk and... I took another sniff. Hmm, apparently, I was going to have to practice my new nappy-changing skills again very soon.

'Renzo, you can't keep picking Gio up every time she makes the slightest sound or she'll never learn to go to sleep on her own.'

I glanced up at the tired murmur from our bed, to catch Jessie yawning. Her face was flushed, the simple cotton nightdress she had been wearing ever since returning from the hospital a week ago had fallen off one shoulder, but despite the censure in her tone I could see the smile in her eyes.

'You are the most beautiful little girl apart of course from your mother, *mia piccola principessa*. As she is the original *Principessa*,' I said, smiling back at my wife.

'Flatterer,' she said, yawning again.

She looked utterly adorable. Of course. And unbearably sexy.

I tramped down manfully on the familiar surge of lust. It would be a while before we could enjoy that part of our relationship again. I forced myself to recall the horror of watching her go through twelve hours of agony to bring our daughter into the world.

As usual it did the trick.

I walked to the bed, careful to slow my stride so that my limp did not jolt my daughter, who I still held securely against my bare chest. I wasn't ready to put her down, especially as she had started to fuss.

There would no doubt be the chance for me to torture myself some more, in a moment, as I watched Jessie feed her—a sight which I had discovered in the past week had to be one of the most deliciously erotic, wonderfully satisfying and yet utterly frustrating sights known to man.

'I think she is hungry again,' I offered, as I perched on the bed.

'You can't be serious?' Jessie frowned, adorably. 'But I literally fed her like half an hour ago,' she said, starting to sound a little perturbed.

I tried not to laugh. I knew she was tired. We both were. Our daughter, it seemed, was not one to observe schedules. And she was almost as attached to her mother's breasts as I was.

'It is just that she has very good taste,' I said, lifting my eyebrows lasciviously. 'Like her papa.'

'Oh god, stop it.' Jessie chuckled, then winced before giving me a playful slap. 'Don't make me laugh, you know I'm still sore.'

'Scusa, cara...' I apologised then leant forward, and gave her a kiss on the nose. Feeling repentant, but also not, because I loved her laugh, almost as much as her breasts. 'Have I told you recently that I adore you, Principessa?' I murmured, as I pulled back, no longer able to keep the love brimming in my heart from spilling out of my mouth. *Again.*

How could I ever have lived without this woman in my life? When she was everything to me now. My lover, my friend, my partner, my wife and also my mistress— I grinned as I thought of how much that word had distressed her once—and now the mother of my daughter. And I hoped, many more babies to come. Although I intended to keep that suggestion to myself for at least a year, to give us both time to recover from the birth.

Famiglia. Family.

A word that had always frightened me—in both Italian and English—before Jessie. Because it had made me think of the mother I had lost. But it meant everything to me now.

'I think you may have mentioned it,' Jessie said, the beaming smile she sent me making me want to say it again. And again. And again.

Giorgia began to wriggle and protest. I looked down at her screwed-up little face and wondered how someone so tiny could be so prefect.

'I can change her and take her for a walk in the grounds if you like,' I said. 'There is some of your milk in the fridge to warm up, yes?'

'It's the middle of the night, Renzo,' Jessie said, as if this was relevant. Her gaze skated down my bare chest, to the boxer shorts I had put on hastily as soon as Gio had begun to snuffle in her basinet. 'And you're virtually naked.'

'It is okay, it is warm out, and you are tired. And Gio and I love our midnight walks,' I said, because it wasn't the first time I'd taken my daughter out in the middle of the night to give her mother a chance to sleep. And the grounds of our home were beautiful this time of year. I liked to tell her all the things we would do in them together when she got a little bigger.

Jessie smile became pensive, as she stared back at me, her gaze so full of love and pride and approval I wanted to bask in it forever. 'You know,' she said softly. 'My mum once told me I should never trust a good-looking guy, especially if he was rich. Just shows how much she knew.'

I frowned. She rarely mentioned her mother. But it always made me sad, and a little angry when she did, because although she had forgiven the woman long ago, I knew I never would.

I placed my hand on her nape, drew her towards me and pressed my forehead to hers with our daughter snuggled between us. 'Your mother was a fool, Jessie,' I whispered, the emotion making my throat close, 'who did not deserve you. But we do.'

She nodded as we drew apart, our daughter's cries becoming louder. 'I'm so glad you know that now,' she said.

Then she lifted the baby out of my arms, and settled her on her breast.

I stretched out on the bed beside her, threw my arm around her shoulder, to tuck them both against my side where they belonged. As I marvelled at the sight of our baby latching on to one plump rosy nipple and sucking voraciously—seriously, it was as if she hadn't been fed in a week—I felt the truth of what I had said spread all the way through my heart.

Jessie was right. I *did* deserve her and my daughter now. And the family we had made together. But that didn't mean I wasn't going to keep earning her love. Because the truth was, there was nothing I enjoyed more.

* * * * *